D1114625

What the critics are saying about John Locke's books!

SAVING RACHEL

"Saving Rachel transcends ordinary storytelling into a class of genius, a stylishly fresh and energetic genre of writing. ...For those who are unfamiliar with Locke's writing and history, this is a perfect way to introduce you to one of the most creative contemporary talents. I'm certainly now one of his fans for life."
~ Gary Sorkin, Pacific Book Review

"A truly spectacular read about an absolutely marvelous con!! Terrific job!!"
~ Claude Bouchard, author, *Vigilante*

"I loved *Saving Rachel*! I could hardly pause for breath! The plot is tight as a drum. The pages flew late into the night; I simply could not stop until the last page!"
~ Winslow Eliot, author, *The Bright Face of Danger*

"Five out of Five Stars! More than a thriller – *Saving Rachel* is a new genre defining excitement!"
~ Steven H. Jackson, author, *Death of a Cure*

"Five out of Five Stars! Dizzying action! *Saving Rachel* moves at a frenzied pace and is bursting with plot twists. I highly recommend it."
~ Melissa Levine, IP Book Reviewers

Saving Rachel is the ultimate adventure with kick-in-the-backside action. Pick up this 'must read' book soon. You will not be disappointed."
~ CK Webb, Webb Weaver Book Reviews

"*Saving Rachel* is a fast—moving thriller, technically complex and a star example of intricate plotting."
~ Elizabeth A. Allen, Clarion Reviews

"While I expected it to be interesting, I didn't expect that I would get so caught up in it! I didn't quit reading until the last page had been consumed!"
~ Joan Ann Hakola, Book Faerie Reviews

"A fenetic, mile-a-minute thriller. Will remind readers of a Hollywood blockbuster full of shakes, rattles, and a high–pitched roar."
~ Kirkus Discoveries, Nielsen Business Media

"Five out of Five Stars! Bravo! Just when you think you have figured it out, you are wrong...and then wrong again...and again!
~ Steven Himes, Ohio

For updates and additional information concerning John Locke's books visit the author's website at:

www.SavingRachel.com

LETHAL PEOPLE

"*Lethal People* stands out as a brazenly smart thriller that's hip and quick. Locke's descriptions pop with a wit and flair that keep the pages turning. It's a fun read that knows when to take itself seriously

~ *BookReview.com*

"Locke has certainly mastered the art of dialogue in this suspenseful tale...To say that this is not your typical mystery/crime series doesn't do the creative spirit of Locke justice. Readers will find that Lethal People is flooded with twists, unexpected characters and action...A page-turner."

~ Holly Christine, *Pittsburgh Book Examiner*

"Five out of Five Stars! The plot moves forward with violent twists that will satisfy readers looking for fast action. Well-defined characters embody the complex dynamics of good and evil. The book's black humor may seem harsh to some but will elicit laughs from readers who get it...This book will please those looking to escape into a story that keeps them guessing until the end."

~ *Margaret Cullison, ForeWord Clarion Review*

"Five out of Five Stars! What a ride! You gotta get on!!! *Lethal People* is a fast moving narrative based on a great character and supporting cast! The book really moves from the first page to the end and caused me to read it in one sitting. I laughed out loud at several of Locke's scenes and had to back up a bit just to make sure that he had really written the words I had just read."

~ *Steven H. Jackson, author, "Death of a Cure"*

"Five out of Five Stars! An exciting thriller pitting killers against killers, *Lethal People* is a choice read, highly recommended."

~ *Midwest Book Reviews*

"A relentlessly entertaining crime novel that's often LOL funny! The action is fast and furious, the dialogue smart, savvy and sexy, and the story is filled with quirky characters and clever surprises."

~ *Gerald Gross, Freelance Editor*

Lethal People is the first installment of the Donovan Creed crime series. Author John Locke has created a bold, intelligent, highly skilled, and humorous lead character. This novel overflows with action while also setting a sturdy foundation for a series of novels that promise exciting and intense plots. Locke's imagination is awesome. The descriptions of Donovan's capabilities as an assassin and agent are vivid and realistic. The humor the author incorporates into the story takes the edge off of Donovan's often unethical and violent behavior. So, even though Donovan is way out there, you have to love this guy. The author also soars in terms of plot and storytelling. Crime novel fans and readers who like to get attached to one intriguing character will love *Lethal People* and yearn for the next book in the series. I highly recommend it.

~ *Melissa Levine, Independent Professional Book Reviewers*

"A good old-fashioned shoot-'em-up adventure story with newfangled weaponry. Well written, energetic and compelling in its quirkiness...an enjoyable page-turner."

~ *Kirkus Discoveries*

For updates and additional information concerning John Locke's books visit the author's website at:

www.SavingRachel.com

Saving
Rachel

BOOKS BY JOHN LOCKE

Lethal People
Lethal Experiment
Saving Rachel
Now & Then

For previews of upcoming books by John Locke and more
information about the author, visit www.**SavingRachel**.com

Saving

Rachel

a Donovan Creed Novel
John Locke

TELEMACHUS
PRESS

This book is a work of fiction. Names, characters, places and incidents are either the product of the author's imagination or are used fictitiously. Any resemblance to actual persons, living or dead, or to actual events or locales is entirely coincidental.

SAVING RACHEL

The publisher does not have any control over and does not assume any responsibility for author or third-party websites or their content.

Cover Art :
Copyright © gettyimages/Martin Barraud

Visit the author website: http://www.SavingRachel.com

Published by: Telemachus Press, LLC
http://www.TelemachusPress.com

ISBN: 9781935670018 (Paperback)
ISBN: 9781935670001 (Hardback)
ISBN: 9781935670025 (eBook)

Printed in the United States of America

10 9 8 7 6 5 4 3 2 1

For my brother, Ricky, whose approval still matters.

Part One

SAM CASE

Chapter 1

MAYBE IT ISN'T fair, but I blame Karen Vogel for what just happened.

I mean, sure, I'd made the first move, and true, I'd plotted her seduction with all the precision of the Normandy invasion. I baited the hook with romantic candlelit dinners, private dining rooms, and elegant wines. I'm the one who made all the promises, bought the clothes, the mushy cards, and glittering jewelry.

But none of this would have happened if Karen Vogel hadn't been so ... gorgeous.

We're in Room 413, Brown Hotel, Louisville, Kentucky, 10:15 am. My twenty-something-year-old conquest lies on the bed watching me through eyes like aquamarine crystals. I'm scrambling into my pants, tucking in my shirt, but those piercing eyes freeze me in place, and I'm like a deer caught in the headlights.

Karen rolls onto her side, props her chin on her fist, and says, "You meant what you said, right, Sam?"

Her toned, athletic body features long legs and a belly so flat I can see two inches down the front of her panties, elevated as they are between two perfect hips. It's a good view, the kind you never get tired of, and I get that feeling again, like I'm riding a lucky wave. I mean, *I just banged Karen Vogel!*

"I meant every last word," I say.

"It was just three words," she laughs, flashing her dazzling White-Cliffs-of-Dover smile, and I'm thinking, *If I couldn't bang Karen, I'd pay serious coin just to watch her brush her teeth!*

Yeah, I know what you're thinking. Go ahead, tell me I'm pathetic. I won't deny it. But I'm the one standing in a hotel room with the semi-naked and infinitely beautiful Karen Vogel, not you. And of course, I'm the one she loves. What? You don't believe me?

Keep reading. I'll prove it.

"I love you, too, Sam," she says. "That's why I did this."

See?

She could have asked me to free Charlie Manson, watch an Oprah film festival, or swim up a ninety-mile-an-hour river of shit to Spain, and I'd have done it. But all I had to do to get in her pants was say, "I love you."

I won't lie. I could tell you I've had my share of beautiful women, and I'd be telling the truth—provided my share is equal to one. So yeah, if I'm brutally honest, I've

2

slept with one beautiful woman before today. And her name is ...

Her name is Rachel.

I don't really want to talk about Rachel right now, but I'll give you a promo and you can be the judge. It's been years since we dated, but in those days, Rachel was coltishly beautiful. She had long brown hair with blond highlights and eyes the color of tupelo honey. Her face was unique, a fabulous contradiction for a young computer geek like me. Angular and beautiful, her face suggested a sophisticated bearing. But her ever-present, enigmatic smile identified her as a keeper of naughty secrets.

At her best, Rachel wasn't in Karen Vogel's league, but honestly, who is? No one I've ever seen. Karen is superstar gorgeous, a French Riviera head-turning, jaw-dropping beauty. So if you're saying Karen's the measuring stick, then Rachel, along with the rest of the planet's women, can't reach it. But with Rachel's looks, you take it all in and maybe you decide the word you're searching for isn't *beautiful*, but something even more special.

She had been adorable.

I see Karen watching me from her perch on the bed. I know I'm supposed to say something to her now, something reassuring, but there's a disconnect between my brain and mouth. So I just keep staring at her, freezing the moment in time, wondering what's going to happen between us from here on out, and realizing we've both upped the ante in our relationship.

I zip my pants, notch my belt, step into my seam-stitched Prada loafers, and wonder if it's true. Do I really love her? *Perhaps not as much as she loves my money,* I think. Then again, it's hard to measure these things when you're only a month into the relationship.

I kiss her good-bye and take the elevator down to the hotel parking garage.

In case you care, I drive an Audi R8, red with a black vertical stripe just back of the cabin. This sexy, low-slung rocket runs a hundred thirty grand and turns heads faster than Paris Hilton crossing her legs in a biker bar.

So I'm in the parking garage, fishing in my pocket for the keyless remote when I hear a crackling sound and—*Christ!*—something zaps my calf muscle from behind. I turn to see what's happened, and the next thing I know, I'm rubbing the back of my neck where it feels like someone stuck me with a hypodermic needle.

I'm groggy, but I feel movement and realize I'm in the back seat of a stretch limo with two guys. The one on the left is a muscle-head; looks like Mr. Clean on steroids. The other guy's a well-dressed older man with slicked-back gray hair. He's wearing a black silk suit with vertical white lines and a white tie. The voice in my head is saying, *Oh shit, this is the real deal,* and the voice is right. This is a full-fledged gangster sitting across from me, and he's just asked me something. Unfortunately, my head is in a fog and I'm still reeling, so I can't quite make out what he said.

Trying to buy time to get my bearings, I say, "I'm sorry. *Who* are you? What did you just say?"

"Your wife," he says.

I look around. *He's talking to me?* His words seem to be coming from deep in a well. *Did he just ask me about my wife?*

4

"What about her?" I ask.

"What's her bra size?"

"Her ... *what?*" I ask. "Who *are* you? What the hell are you talking about?"

He sits there in silence, with no hint of a smile.

I pat my pocket instinctively, feeling for my cell phone. Then I remember I left it in the car so I wouldn't be disturbed while seducing Karen. Nothing kills the mood faster than a phone call, right?

Unless you're interrupted by a gangster. That would be worse.

I'm trying to remain calm, hoping to clear my head of this thick, fuzzy feeling. I look out the window and see we're only about eight blocks from the hotel. We're moving slowly, making our way down Liberty Street. I look out the window and see a homeless guy sitting on the curb, his back propped against a street lamp. He's wearing a red corduroy jacket and holding a sign in his lap that says, "Stop Offering Me Work!" I wonder briefly if this is some sort of marketing ploy on his part, and it strikes me I've got more important things to worry about, like what the hell is going on. I'm afraid to stare at the gangster or Mr. Clean, so I continue looking out the window. We're picking up speed now. I watch us pass a heart rehab clinic, an office building with a Starbucks on the first floor, a Thornton's gas station, and then it's under the interstate and up the ramp onto the expressway, heading east.

"Where are you *taking* me?" I ask.

The well-dressed *Sopranos* wannabe waves his hand. "Here's your problem: you ask too many questions. I ask a simple question, you ask me two in return. So I'm gonna try again," he says. "What's Rachel's bra size?"

I go cold inside. *This mobster knows my wife's name?*

If we're being completely honest, I should admit that after dating Rachel six years ago, I married her. And while she's no longer coltish or enigmatic, I still love her very much. I know you'll find this hard to believe, given my recent activities with Karen Vogel and having heard me profess my love for her back in the hotel room. You need to understand—well, you don't need to understand it at all. But I'd like to explain. Wooing and bedding Karen has nothing to do with loving Rachel. I need—I *crave*—the attention, the ... appreciation. It's been such a long time since Rachel was impressed by anything I'd accomplished. Do you have any idea what it's like to invent something no one has ever thought of before? Something only a handful of people in the world even *know* about?

No, of course you don't. No offense, but if you'd done that, you'd be telling your own story right now instead of reading mine.

What did I do that's so special?

Drum roll, please ... I created a computer program that makes it impossible to track money. Bear with me, this is a bigger deal than you might think. If you deposit, say, a hundred million dollars in a checking account, my program splits that sum into a hundred different bundles and shoots them at bullet speed to different banks all over the world every twenty minutes. The only way to stop the transfers is to enter a sixteen-digit code into my Web site. When that happens, the bundles park themselves in their current location until a second code, known only to my clients, is entered. Then the bundles reassemble into the client's original checking account. I only have eighteen clients, but they each pay me ten thousand a month to keep their money safe from prying eyes.

We all sit and look at each other as the limo switches lanes and accelerates onto I-64. After a moment of silence, the gangster says, "You love your wife, Sam?"

Do I love my wife?

"Of course I love her," I say, wondering where this is going. *Does he know about Karen? Could he possibly know about the affair?*

"You love your wife, you oughta know her bra size," he says.

I allow myself to relax the slightest bit. At least this isn't about Karen. I give him a defiant stare. *Who the hell does he think he is?* If not for the complete absence of humor, I'd have sworn this was all a big, unfunny joke. In the background, I hear the limo driver talking softly into a wireless phone device. "Four minutes," is the only thing I hear him say clearly.

Four minutes? Till what?

Chapter 2

THE GANGSTER'S VOICE contains no hint of inflection. "Rachel's bra size, Sam," he says. "Last chance."

I shout, "Fuck you!"

We pull off the interstate and turn onto Cannons Lane, heading for Seneca Park.

"Are you trying to kidnap me?" I ask, wondering why it took so long for this happy thought to enter my brain. They're not answering, but it doesn't *feel* like a kidnapping— not that I've ever been involved in one. But no, whatever this is, it isn't a kidnapping. If it were, they'd be kidnapping Rachel, not me. They'd kidnap her and hit me up for the ransom. And if they knew what I did for a living, we'd be talking seven figures. Anyway, the only demand I'd received so far was my wife's bra size. Rachel's great looking, but I seriously doubt this bit of personal information warrants my kidnapping.

My name—Sam Case—isn't well-known, even in Louisville. Even our closest friends have no idea what I do. They
think I'm a computer whiz, a guy who corrects the glitches
and circular references that plague new software applications
prior to launch. I do that from time to time, and those jobs
bring in a quarter mil each year, which is nothing to sneeze
at. But even Rachel doesn't understand what I really do. Of
course I tried to explain it to her a hundred times. When
you've done something amazing, you can't wait to tell your
wife, right? I put in thousands of hours, poured my heart
and soul into this, and the day I finally made it work, I tried
to turn it into a big night. I planned a huge celebration; I
couldn't wait to see the look of pride and admiration in her
eyes. But she couldn't have cared less. To her, it was another
possible paycheck at best. Lockdown T3, that's the name of
my electronic money program, the one that constantly shifts
funds from one bank to another, all over the world, three
times per hour, seven days a week.

Rachel barely made an effort to comprehend it. Two
minutes into the explanation, she goes, "How can that possibly be true? Banks are closed on weekends and holidays."

"It doesn't matter if American banks are closed on
certain days," I say. "It's always the next day somewhere in
the world—or the previous day."

"You're hysterical," she says.

"Hysterical?" Of all the comments she could have made,
who'd have guessed she'd come up with that? Then she
says—I shit you not, "Pass the salt, please."

The appearance and demeanor of the gangster sitting
across from me suggests serious wealth, but not at the level

sufficient to make my client list—not that I'm seeking new clients. He appears cool and calm. His voice comes across in a practiced, matter-of-fact tone, and he's trying for sophisticated, but not quite pulling it off. His hands are meaty, his knuckles gnarled, and I see traces of scar tissue around both eyes, remnants of battles waged and won. This man strikes me as one who fought and clawed his way to the top of a very dangerous ladder. Though he is middle-aged and unarmed, something about him makes him more frightening than the muscle-head sitting beside him.

Speaking of the muscle-head, I notice he hasn't so much as twitched the entire time I've been conscious in the car. He's a beast of a man with a sheath of muscles that bullies the fibers of his suit. He has a dull, *don't-give-a-shit* look that marks him as a primitive man, one who could snap at any moment and morph into *the Incredible Hulk*.

I look away and quickly look back to see if he flinches. He does not. He just continues staring at me through vacant, unblinking, reptilian eyes—as if daring me to venture just a wee bit closer so he can feed.

"Rachel's got a sister," the gangster says, "name of Mary."

I look at him but say nothing.

"I'm telling you this about Mary because I want you to know I expect answers from you, regardless of the question. You might think the question is silly or personal or ... whatcha call ... irrelevant to the situation at hand. But I don't give a shit what you think about my questions. They will be answered, or there will be ... whatcha call ... consequences."

"Like what?" I sneer, showing him my tough side. I flex a bit.

He sighs. "Oh, please."

With that, the driver pulls up to the curb near the jogging trail and parks the car. He keeps the engine running.

The gangster shakes his head from side to side, pretending to be overcome by a heavy sadness. He says, "Sam, you disappoint me. It's clear you're not ready for the discussion I wanted us to have. So for now, I'm gonna let you go."

I blink a couple of times and rub my calf to get the blood flowing. From the moment I entered the parking garage, nothing has made a lick of sense. But I figure if I can get out of the car in one piece, maybe I can find my way back to the planet Earth. I wonder if he's teasing me or if this is someone's sick idea of a joke. Either way, if he intends to let me go, I intend to exit the car sprinting.

"We'll wait here a minute," the gangster says, "in case you want to catch a ride back to the hotel with us."

Fat chance.

To the driver, he says, "Turn the car around, and unlock the door."

When that's done, he says, "Okay, Sam, off you go."

I've always lived my life by a simple rule: don't spend more time in a limo with a crazed gangster and a *T. rex* than you have to. I follow my own advice and jump out of the car where the jogging trail loops between Rock Creek and Reece. I hit the ground running with a specific destination in mind and move toward it with all the speed I can extract from my legs.

I'm running to the cop on Reece, the one who's talking to Rachel's sister, Mary.

I'm full throttle now, yelling and waving my arms like a castaway trying to flag down a passing ship. They turn toward me, and several things happen all at once: A look of surprise registers in Mary's face as she recognizes me. A shot rings out. Mary falls to the ground. The cop hits the street and starts radioing for help. I stop in my tracks. The cop quick-crawls to Mary to check her pulse.

Another shot rings out.

The policeman's head explodes.

An engine revs, a car door slams in the distance, and tires squeal on pavement as an Audi R8, red with a black vertical stripe, races away from the scene.

Chapter 3

I NEED TO ... what? Run for cover? Run to Mary's side? Call Rachel? Get help? *What the hell is going on?* I feel a surge of panic overloading my brain circuits. My feet seem bolted to the ground, and I remain this way until the screaming starts.

I look around. People are pointing at me, screaming the two words I don't want to hear: *"Get him!"*

I hold up my hands in protest. "It wasn't me!" I yelp. Why would they even *think* that? I'm her brother-in-law. They couldn't possibly think I was involved in the shooting. I don't even have a gun, for Chrissake.

I'm selling, but the park people aren't buying. Worse, they're becoming a mob. A mob full of angry, athletic men and women who suddenly start running toward me, converging on my position at breakneck speed from both sides of the field.

I turn around to check for the limo and see it hasn't moved. I put my faith in my legs and make an all-out burst, hoping to get back to the car before the crowd can overtake me. While I run, I shield my face to make it harder for them to identify me later.

The bad news is most of the younger guys are lean runner-types and there's no way I'm going to outrun them in a normal footrace. The good news is I'm in great shape, I have the lead and the angle, and this isn't a normal footrace; it's life and death.

I press on.

Now the limo is less than a hundred yards away, and I'm closing fast. But my breath is coming quicker and my lungs start to ache. The faster runners close in on me like a pack of jackals. *What made them so flippin' brave all of a sudden? Sheer numbers? The fact that I'm unarmed?*

Two runners appear out of nowhere, cutting me off. I spin around. There's no place to go, nowhere to hide. The park people slow down and begin forming a circle around me. I put my hands up, ready to surrender.

What happens next seems to unfold in slow motion. Behind the runners, I see the limo door open. Mr. Clean emerges with an enormous gun. He slowly lifts it, takes aim, and seamlessly fires two shots that strike both of my would-be captors in the back of the head. My eyes are transfixed on his face as he watches them fall, and I can tell you there is no change in his expression. He could be watching two men die, watching traffic, or watching paint dry. Then Mr. Clean lowers his gun, turns, and climbs back into the limo.

The stunned mob veers away from me in a single motion, like a school of fish encountering a big-eyed predator. Somewhere behind me, a woman shrieks. The two runners between me and the car appear to be dead. I'm horrified, but not so horrified that I can't hurdle their bodies and run to the open door of the waiting limo.

Inside, Mr. Clean is sitting, pointing his gun at my face. I start to enter the vehicle, but Mr. Clean cocks the hammer. I freeze where I am, which is halfway in and halfway out.

The crowd behind me is starting to reconsider their retreat, a decision that bodes poorly for me. Mr. Clean places his index finger on the trigger, and that bodes worse.

The gangster says, "You need a lift?"

"I do," I say.

The gangster says nothing. Behind me, I feel the crowd moving toward the car, slowly at first, like *Night of the Living Dead*, but with a growing confidence that the shooting might be over.

"May I please have a ride?" I say.

No response.

Then it hits me. "Thirty-two B," I say. "Rachel's bra size."

The gangster says, "Jump in."

The driver guns the engine, and the big tires squeal as we roar out of Seneca Park. We hit the freeway doing ninety and head back downtown, toward the hotel where Karen Vogel and I had sex less than thirty minutes ago.

Chapter 4

I GAG AND retch, but manage not to throw up in the limo. When I'm able to speak, I shout everything that's on my mind. "You killed Mary! *Oh, my God!* And the others! What the hell is going on? What do you want from me? And what the fuck does Rachel have to do with this?"

The mobster remains calm in the face of my outburst.

"You brought this on yourself," he says. "Maybe you answered my question ten minutes ago ..." He turns his palms up and shakes his head. "... none of this happens."

My brain cells spin like slot-machine tumblers as I try to process his words. If I heard him correctly, this goomba wants me to believe that the closely guarded secret of my wife's small titties has caused her sister's death. If he'd said he played pinochle every Tuesday with an eggplant, that would make more sense.

"You're insane!" I shout. "You're freaking insane!" The tremor in my voice tells me I'm shaking.

He shrugs. "Don't talk for a minute," he says. "You been through a lot just now. Take a deep breath and think about some things, like how you're not going to tell anyone about the time we spent together today."

I look at him—and not for the first time—as though he's lost his mind. Of course I'm going to tell! I'm going to tell anyone who will listen. I might put an ad in the paper about it, maybe post a billboard or set up a Web site.

"I see the wheels turning," he says. "Maybe it's best I kill you now."

I stop in mid-thought and show a "no wheels are turning" look to the guy who just had my sister-in-law whacked, along with three other people, including a cop. *Holy shit!* It just hit me. *These guys killed a cop!*

"I'd rather keep my mouth shut than die," I say, trying to calm down.

We ride in silence until I say, "What do you want from me?"

"Listen to yourself," he says, "going on again with the questions. Look, we'll talk again soon. You'll call me when the time is right."

"*Call* you? I don't even know who you are. You're going to give me your phone number?"

"Sometime soon, you'll pick up the phone. I'll be on the line."

The one thing I know for certain is he doesn't know how telephones work.

To the driver, he says, "Hand me the bag."

The driver picks up a pink *Victoria's Secret* bag with his right hand and passes it back to Mr. Clean, who in turn hands it to the gangster.

"I'll tell you one last time," the gangster says. His voice is steady, his words firm and measured. "Don't speak of this to anyone, not even Rachel. Say, 'Yes, sir.'"

"Yes, sir."

He hands me the Victoria's Secret bag. "Speaking of Rachel," he says, "I got her a little present. A ... whatcha call ... replacement."

I open the bag and push the pink-and-white tissue paper aside. I remove the gift, wondering what he means by "replacement." The tag says, "Perfect One, TM, Full-Coverage Bra." It also says, "Padded, Level 1, Size 32 B."

I look at the gangster.

"You think she'll like it?" he says.

Chapter 5

THEY DROP ME off a block from the hotel, and I'm wondering how many red Audi R8s there could possibly be in Louisville, Kentucky, and it suddenly dawns on me to check my pockets to see if my keys are there. I do, and they're not.

I walk with purpose to the hotel parking lot, wondering how long it will take the media to post my name and photograph on TV. The cops are probably swamped with eyewitness accounts, not to mention the cell phone videos that are no doubt being posted on YouTube as we speak.

How much trouble can I be in? I wonder. I didn't shoot anyone, and no one in the park could claim I had. But multiple witnesses saw me approach all four people just before they were shot. Two of the gunshots were fired from the area where my car was parked—or at least a car that looked like mine. The other two were fired by Mr. Clean, with whom I was seen escaping the scene. So, while no one can think I'm solely responsible for the murders, I'm far more than "a person of interest," as the police like to say.

I know it's too early for the manhunt to have reached downtown Louisville, but I can't help feeling as though everyone is staring at me. When I round the corner into the parking garage, I see my car right where I'd left it. I fling the door open, jump in and instinctively reach beneath the driver's seat, where I find an envelope. Inside are two items: my keys and a photograph. I'm not expecting the photograph, or what it depicts, so it takes a half second to register in my brain.

I look at the photo and fill the car with a sudden gasping sound. I stare at the photograph in disbelief. I flip it over, but there's nothing written on the back. I turn it again, and the computer in my head makes a note that today's date has been electronically stamped on the bottom right-hand corner, along with the time: 8:46 am. My breath comes quickly. My fingers tremble so violently I drop the photo. As it falls, the edge catches my knee, and the photograph is sent skittering deep into the leg well, near the brake pedal. Nausea floods my gut. I'll retrieve the picture in a few seconds, but right now, I'm feeling sick. I think about what I saw and start shuddering. It's the most unsettling image I've ever seen in my life, and no matter how strained our relationship has been recently, no matter how far we've grown apart these past few months, Rachel and I are still connected in all the ways that truly count, and I've got to get home to her. I've got to save Rachel, and I will.

But first, I have to call the police.

Chapter 6

I CAN THINK of a million reasons not to call the cops—the most serious one being the gangster's warning—but I'm in over my head. This is no longer about me, about some gangster trying to set me up for Mary's murder. This is about saving Rachel.

I grip my fingers around my cell phone and start to dial 911. Before I get the third digit pressed, the passenger door flies open, startling me. It's Karen Vogel. She climbs in, saying, "What're you doing here? You left a long time ago. I *saw* you!"

"Wait—why are *you* still here?" I say, trying to turn the tables on her.

"I took a shower," she says, eyeing me suspiciously. "What's *your* story?"

It's a good question, one for which bullshit is the only answer.

"I just pulled up. I had to hold you one more time," I lie shamelessly.

"Aww, Sam. That's so sweet!"

It was sweet. I make a note to remember the line. Maybe it will work on Rachel before they throw the switch on me for conspiracy to murder her sister.

"What's in the bag?" she says.

"Bag?"

"The Victoria's Secret bag in the backseat."

"Oh that. It's a present."

"For me?"

"Of course for you!" My lies are on autopilot, beyond my control. At this point, I'll do or say anything to get home. Rachel needs me.

"You left here to go buy me something? And then you drove all the way back to give it to me in person? Oh ... my ... God!"

She leans over and gives me a big kiss on the mouth, the kind of kiss I'd give anything to get—some other time, but not now. Rachel needs me. I can't believe I'm sitting here, still going through the motions with Karen. *What kind of jerk would do that?* I wonder and then mentally answer my own question. *The kind of jerk who has a nagging feeling in the back of his mind that somehow Karen Vogel might be involved.* In my gut, I'm not ready to believe Karen is mixed up in all this, but how else can I explain our Beauty-and-the-Beast love story? *I mean, come on, Karen Vogel? In love with not Christian Bale or Matthew McConaughey or Colin Farrell but me?*

Karen snatches the Vicky's Secret bag from the backseat, opens it, and says, "Oh, Sam, I *love* it!"

"You do?"

She holds it up in front of her, and I see her expression change ever so slightly, like a thin cloud passing briefly across the sun.

"Yes, but ... it's a bit small for me, don't you think?"

I look at the label and pretend I'm shocked. "I'm so sorry," I say. "I'll exchange it immediately. I can't believe they wrapped the wrong size. Guess I was in such a hurry to get back before you left."

"I'm sorry," she says. "It really is a wonderful gift. And it means the world to me that you went to all this trouble."

I'm trying to say all the right things to Karen but my pulse is pounding the drum line from "Wipe Out" in my ears. I study Karen's face with full knowledge that I make my living by reading computer code, not people. So I really stare at her and come away with this: if there's any guile in Karen's face or body language, I can't find it. Either she's the greatest actress in the world, or she's completely innocent in this whole gangster/Mary/Rachel thing. I'm leaning toward her being innocent, but I can't dwell on it. I've wasted enough time sitting in my car. Rachel needs me. Now! I make a show of looking at my watch. "I've got to run," I say.

"Me too. I'm going in to work after all."

"You called in sick," I say.

"I'll tell them I got better. I'd rather keep half a sick day for the next time." She gives me a wink.

I nod.

She whispers, "I love you, Sam."

She kisses me again. Then she opens her door, but first, we do that thing where we slowly break away from each other until just our fingertips are touching. I'm thinking, *God, I'm pathetic.* Finally, mercifully, she's gone. I fire the ignition. Before I blast off, I take a deep breath and look at the photograph again.

In it, Rachel is lying spread-eagle on her back on our kitchen floor. She's blindfolded. Her hands and feet are tied to eyebolts that have been screwed into the floorboards. She's wearing a white bra and black panties, nothing more. She has some sort of ball in her mouth, like the kind you'd see in a low-grade bondage movie.

On her bra cups, written in thick, indelible ink, are the letters "K" and "V."

If that doesn't stand for Karen Vogel, I'm out of ideas.

Chapter 7

TRAFFIC IN DOWNTOWN Louisville is only heavy at noon and five, and noon is a half hour away. By then, I'll be at Rachel's side or in police custody, and I'm not sure which is safer.

I make short work of the downtown area, hit the interstate ramp, kick the Audi into third, and catch rubber out of the turn. I shift again and jam the gas pedal till I hear the engine whine. I shift to fifth, flying. I'm flying! But my mind is flying faster.

Someone has molested my wife, unless she woke up wearing a white bra and black panties. I try to think. Did she? I rewound the morning in my head. She was sleeping when I left. What about last night? *Think!* Last night, I came into the bathroom, and—

Shit! I swerve and change lanes, barely missing the car in front of me. I'd misjudged its speed. I look at the needle. I've slowed to one-ten. *Jesus!*

Okay, so last night, she's at her makeup desk in the bathroom. She's sitting there, her back to me as I enter the room to brush my teeth. She's just showered and still has a towel on her head. She's got another towel draped around her shoulders; she's not wearing a bra. And she ... she *does* have on black panties. Okay, so it's possible she put on a white bra. Wait—no, it's not possible. She wears a flannel nightshirt to bed, no bra. This morning, I get up and get dressed, and she's still asleep in her upstairs bedroom. So, she does what? Wakes up after I leave, starts getting dressed, right? Maybe she puts on the white bra and starts getting dressed, but someone breaks in and—

No. I force myself away from that scenario. Maybe she's sleeping when they break in. They overpower her. No, that's even worse. I stop concentrating on how they got her bound and gagged and into the bra and focus instead on *why*.

Why would they write "K" and "V" on her cups? It's a reference to Karen Vogel, nothing could be more obvious. In the photograph, Rachel is blindfolded. Does that mean she doesn't know what they wrote on her bra? If so, I'll have to come up with a plan to get her bra off before she sees it.

Excuse me?

I slap my forehead to remind myself to stop being a jerk. This is my wife. She's lying on the floor. She's scared to death. She's bound and gagged, and—

And blindfolded. There it is again. I can't get my mind off the blindfold.

My best guess is Rachel doesn't know about Karen. The "K" and "V" are a warning to me. If I don't do what they want, they'll tell Rachel about the affair.

But what do they want me to do?

They've never said.

I wonder if they have pictures. I wonder again if Karen could have set me up. I've only known her a month. How well can you possibly know someone in just a month? I mean, Karen's been with me the same month and doesn't know I'm married, right? But what if she *does* know about Rachel? Would she want to punish me for lying to her?

Possibly.

But is she capable of murder?

No. But this isn't about the affair. If Karen found out I was married, she'd throw a shit fit, sure. But she wouldn't do anything that would result in the death of my wife's sister or a policeman.

Unless ...

What is it they always say in the movies?

Follow the money.

Good advice, that. Because this is almost certainly about the money, and not just *my* money, I'm beginning to suspect, but the money I move for my clients.

One of the lanes is closed up ahead, and I'm forced to downshift to sixty, which gives me more time to think.

Maybe I'm coming at it the wrong way. Maybe the gangster found out about Lockdown T3 and hired Karen Vogel to be receptive to my advances. Maybe he figured if Karen got close enough, I'd give her details about my operation. If that's it, she's done a helluva job, because other than the standard, "What do you do for a living?" Karen's hardly mentioned my business.

But I have.

I've told her plenty.

That's me, Mr. Big Shot, trying to impress Karen from day one and throughout the whole courtship, making sure she knows how special I am, how lucky she is to be with me, how clever, rich, and successful I am, what I did to get that way, and how it works. So yeah, I told her plenty—not enough to breach my security, but certainly enough to pique her interest on behalf of her gangster friend.

Listen to me, "gangster friend." We're talking about Karen Vogel here, not Vicky Gotti.

My inner voice starts in on me. *Oh really? Then what about all the coincidences?* I list them: One, at the exact time I'm in the hotel room with Karen, someone is photographing my wife on the kitchen floor wearing a bra with Karen's initials. Two, when I leave Karen's hotel room, a gangster attacks me in the hotel garage and takes me to a park. Three, it's not just any park, but the park where Rachel's sister happens to be.

So of course Karen is involved. But who came first, Karen or the gangster?

It had to be Karen.

Maybe she didn't know the gangster before I started running my mouth, but after hearing my stories, she must have started formulating a plan. A girl like Karen wouldn't know how to do it herself, but she probably knows some shady character who has the right connections. Meaning, there could be several, possibly a bunch of people involved in the plan—which makes sense. After all, I'm floating billions of dollars for my clients, not just millions.

My inner voice is relentless. *Great work, big man. You thought you seduced Karen Vogel, but she played you and you fell for it like the pathetic little worm you are! Now your sister-in-law is dead, your wife's in danger, your marriage is down the toilet, the cops are after you—oh, and by the way, if she succeeds in getting you to steal money from your clients ... well, you know what kind of men you're dealing with. There is no solution, no outcome that's going to get you back to the life you used to have. Face it, you're ...*

I'm fucked.

Unless ...

Unless ...

Unless I kill her.

Right, just listen to yourself. Like you've got the guts to kill someone! But even if you did, you'd have to kill the gangster and Mr. Clean as well. Think you're up for the job, big man?

I want to pull over and throw up.

That beautiful bitch set me up!

My life is totally fucked. Everything I've built, everything I've worked for has been flushed down the toilet in a month's time. I can't believe I put myself and the people I care about into this situation. And for what: a little trim. *Son of a bitch!* What the hell am I going to do?

You can start by saving Rachel, you stupid prick.

I'm close to my exit but stuck behind an eighteen-wheeler. I want to pass him, but there's a Saab clinging to the speed limit in the left lane. I'll have to sit tight till I reach the turn.

My focus shifts to Mary and the policeman and the joggers from the park. Why were they shot? How did the gangster know Mary would be there? Could Karen possibly be involved in the park thing? Though I'm resigning myself to the fact that she used me and may have ruined my life, I'm still having trouble believing she's a cold, calculating killer.

But Karen almost has to be involved to some extent. Could she have formulated the extortion plan? If she did, I wonder if maybe the gangster hijacked her plan. He told me he wanted me to know he means business. Kidnapping me and stealing my car would have convinced me of that. If he's trying to extort money from me, why not give a warning first or make some sort of demand?

Why would he kill Mary? She's completely innocent.

My inner voice says, *What if Mary was in on it? What if she changed her mind at the last minute and they killed her to keep her quiet?*

My inner voice always assumes the worst. But no, Mary's a good— was a good friend. I always suspected she liked me far more than she liked her own sister. She wouldn't have turned on me for the money.

But my inner voice isn't through with me. It hits me below the belt with a question that sends me reeling: *What if Rachel is involved?*

Chapter 8

I THINK ABOUT that. If Rachel found out about Karen, she'd blow a gasket. She'd demand a divorce. But all we'd be splitting is our highly mortgaged mansion and the small amount I earn legally—not enough. So Mary suggests killing me, but Rachel says killing me would do her no good, since all my income is generated by what I do personally. If I were dead, all she'd get is the small amount of money in our bank account. So they hatch a plan to extort money from me. Mary gets a gangster involved, and he kills her to keep her quiet.

If this is how it went down, Rachel wouldn't know that Mary had been killed.

I shake off these thoughts. In my heart, I don't believe Rachel or Mary had anything to do with today's horrible events. I think Karen started something that quickly got out of control, and as a result, Mary's dead and Rachel is lying on the floor in my kitchen.

I wonder what happened to Rachel. I wonder who did it and why. I speed up at the Blankenbaker exit, squealing my tires on the wide, looping ramp. I glance at my watch. I'm sure she's not hurt. Scared, sure, that's a given. But they didn't hurt her. They wouldn't hurt Rachel.

Not until they get the money.

I make the light and shift into third. The gangster bought Rachel a replacement bra. He wouldn't have done that unless he'd expected her to be able to wear it.

Unless it's for her burial.

I feel the stomach juices boiling in my gut. I look at my watch again. I'll know what happened to Rachel in about … four minutes.

This is not about the affair. *Follow the money.* They killed Mary to show me what they're capable of. They physically manipulated and photographed my wife to demonstrate their ability to invade my house. The "K" and "V" prove they have something on me, something that can be used to disrupt my marriage.

It's a lot to take in, but don't kid yourself, Sammy Boy; this is about the money. They decided a warning wouldn't do. A demand wouldn't have the proper impact. So they're putting on a show of violence and threats, and the implication is obvious: play ball and we won't tell Rachel about Karen; play ball and Rachel gets to live.

Okay, so if I'm right, if this is a warning, Rachel is probably okay. Maybe she's been drugged, and if so, I'll be able to untie her, destroy the bra, and get her back in bed. But yes, they are definitely serious. They've already killed

Mary. Have I fully comprehended the enormity of that statement? They've killed Rachel's sister, murdered her in cold blood, right before my eyes.

I'm two blocks away from my wife now, and my first thought is to circle the block and make sure no one is waiting for me. Then I realize how stupid this sounds because I've still got the only red Audi R8 in town. If they've put me at the scene, I'm toast, whether I circle the block or not.

I roar into my driveway, press the remote door button, and enter the garage. I press the button again to close the door behind me. No sense in making it too easy for the cops to know I'm home.

I climb the four steps to the landing, enter the code to unlock the door, and hit the hall running. My house is huge—13,000 square feet—but the kitchen is only steps away. I turn into the opening and see the large granite island in the center of the room. The island is four feet high, fourteen feet long, and six feet wide. It's called a granite island, but only the top is granite. The base is wood, with cabinets on this side and bar stools on the other. From the angle of the photograph, I know that Rachel is lying on the other side, just past the bar stools, hidden from my current view.

I suddenly think, *What if someone is crouching down, waiting there for me?*

Before I go to her, I call out, "Rachel?"

I don't expect her to answer in anything but a muffled voice, but I'm more than a little alarmed to receive no response at all.

I raise my voice and try again, but again, I'm met with an eerie silence.

I hesitate. The voice inside my head screams, *It's a trap!* I think about it a moment. *What should I do? I can't save Rachel if I'm dead.* The more I think about it, the more I believe this situation does have all the earmarks of a trap. But if it's a trap, why not just jump up from behind the island and riddle my body with bullets?

Then I think, *Rachel could be lying there, dying. They could have beaten her and left her to die. Or maybe they tied the gag too tight and she's choked to death.*

This is Rachel, the woman I married. Why would anyone want to punish her?

This is not about Rachel. It's about Lockdown T3. Someone wants the codes.

Whatever's happened to Rachel, I now realize it's my fault. I've brought this on her. This has to do with me and the people I deal with, my "prized" client list of drug lords; terrorists; a crazed, homicidal quadriplegic; a professional assassin ...

Ours is a three-million-dollar house, not counting the furniture. When we designed it, there were certain things we both wanted, like the upstairs girl's and boy's rooms. Both would have lofts and deep, walk-in closets with secret rooms. This was years ago when we still dreamed about having children, back when we were having sex on a more or less regular basis. One of the things we didn't agree on was this enormous pile of granite in the kitchen. From the initial concept drawing, I thought it a monstrosity, but I'd given Rachel my word she could design the kitchen and family room, and I stuck to it.

We'd been counting on this dream house to bring us together, and I didn't want something as silly as a granite kitchen island to keep us apart. Here we are, two years later, and it's standing between us again, perhaps for the last time. I dread turning the corner, terrified of what I might see.

Then I think, *A sedative! That's it! They gave her a sedative, drew the "K" and "V" on her cups while she was knocked out. A sedative could easily last three and a half hours.* It makes sense, such perfect sense that I put aside my fear and start to circle the granite island. Though I know Rachel's okay, I have a pretty good idea what I'll find on the other side, how she'll look, so I take a deep breath and set my jaw.

But I'm wrong.

Oh, am I wrong!

Of all the things I expected to see on the floor on the other side of the island, this shocks me the most.

What I see is ...

Chapter 9

NOTHING! NO RACHEL.

Could she have gotten up somehow, untied herself? I run through the house, shouting her name.

Think!

I run back to the garage and notice for the first time that her car isn't there. I call her cell phone.

No answer.

Think!

Lockdown T3. Someone's kidnapped, Rachel. They want the codes.

I go to my desk, power up my computer, navigate to the key-code page. I pause with my hand above the mouse.

This is dangerous. Very dangerous. But I have to see if anyone has been trying to access my clients.

I click the cursor into the first space: Creed, Donovan. I type in the sixteen digits and press enter.

The house phone rings. Do I dare answer it? I have to. "Hello?"

"Sam, what do you want? I'm about to go to lunch."

My mind is sputtering.

It's Rachel.

I'm so startled I can't think of anything to say.

"Lunch, Sam. I've only got an hour, remember?"

"Uh, are you okay?"

She sighs. "What are you doing home? Are you sick?"

"Uh, no, I'm good. Had to pick up some work papers."

She pauses. "Is this about last night?"

Last night? What happened last night?

"What happened last night?" I ask.

"Nothing. That's the point. No good night, no hug, no nothing. I just figured you were all wrapped up in your little dream world. As usual."

This is, of course, total bullshit.

Rachel has a way of transferring her thoughts and actions onto me. In fact, *she's* the one who had no interest in saying good night last night. Now that I think about it, I remember she'd been pacing the floor from the time I'd gotten home to the time she went to bed. When I walked into the kitchen last night, she'd been on her cell phone, agitated. I saw her try to make a call over and over, though she never left a message. At one point, she'd been in her closet with the door closed. When I entered, I saw her sitting on the floor, eyes filled with tears, cell phone in her lap. I'd asked what was going on. She'd told me to leave her alone.

So it was Rachel who was responsible for last night, not me. But none of this matters now. She's okay. Rachel's ...

"I'm sorry," I say. "About last night. Look, I'm—" I thought about the time stamp on the photograph: 8:46 am. "What time did you get to work today?"

She pauses. "Sam, what's going on?"

I can't think of any reason to give for asking the question. So I say nothing. Finally, she answers. "I got here the same time I always do, eight thirty."

I recover slightly. "I'm ... I'm just glad you're okay."

"Why wouldn't I be?"

I start to answer, but when I think about the conversation from her point of view, I sound like an idiot. Instead, I just say, "I love you. Have a good lunch."

We hang up. If she's confused about the call, I'm dumbfounded. I take a minute to look closely at the floor. There are no holes in the wood. There have to be holes, right? From where they screwed in the eyebolts when they tied Rachel down? I wonder if maybe I had the angle all wrong. Maybe the picture was taken on the front side of the island. I check it and the entire surrounding area.

No holes.

I go to the car, retrieve the photograph, bring it back inside, and check it carefully. I get on my hands and knees and brush the floor with the heel of my hand, thinking maybe they'd filled the holes with some type of epoxy that appears invisible when dry. But I find nothing. I briefly wonder if Rachel found out about Karen Vogel and decided to stage the whole thing. If so, who bound her and took the photo?

No, that whole line of thought is crazy. Rachel wouldn't know how to put all this together, and anyway, Rachel isn't the type. If she knew about Karen, she'd be in my face about it.

But if Rachel had nothing to do with it, what the hell's going on?

It finally hits me: *they used a body double.*

Then, by extension, I think, *Could they have used a body double for Mary? And if so, why?*

I think about calling Mary and quickly discard the idea. If she answers, what reason could I give for calling? And if she's dead, why would I want my number among her recent calls in the phone records? I decide to work with what I have: a photograph of a body double, wearing a white bra, with the letters "K" and "V" on the cups.

I go back to my idea that the "K" and "V" are a warning to me. If that's the case, maybe the bra is hidden somewhere in the house, possibly in the laundry basket or among Rachel's things. I can't take the chance that Rachel will come home, find the bra, and confront me with the initials.

I rush to her closet and check through her drawers but come up empty. I look in her laundry basket. Nothing. I run back down the hall to the laundry room.

Then I hear the front doorbell ring.

Chapter 10

I PEER OUT the laundry room window and freeze. Two guys in suits are standing at the front door. I look behind them, to the driveway, and spot a black sedan, one that looks very much like the standard detective cars you see on TV. They ring the bell again and wait twenty seconds. Then, they knock on the door, loudly. I see one of them sweep the windows with his eyes. Before he can see me, I drop to the floor and make my way to the little cubby where we keep the large laundry bag, the one that has different sections for sorting colors and fabrics.

The bag is on a metal frame and has wheels. I roll it out of the cubby and work my way behind it. I reach into the laundry bag and pull out an armful of dirty clothes and cover myself as best I can. If the detectives are honest, I'm safe. If not, if they break in and search the place, I'm caught. A couple minutes pass. More ringing, more knocking, and suddenly, a knock from the back door, ten feet from my hiding place, scares the shit out of me.

"Mr. Case?" a man's voice says.

"Sam?" It comes at me again. "We need to speak with you. We need to talk about what happened at Seneca Park."

That said, he circles to the back of the house, where he has to open a gate and climb the patio steps if he wants to knock on the back door. He does. It strikes me that if Rachel had been lying behind the island, he'd be able to see her clearly from the patio door. I hear yet another burst from the doorbell, which tells me the first guy is still on the front porch. They spend five minutes trying to find someone home, and then everything goes silent.

Probably going to get a search warrant.

I carefully climb out from under the pile of laundry, and as I do, my arm gets hooked up in the strap from a white bra with the letters "K" and "V" written on the cups in heavy black marker ink. I hang onto it while peering through the window, checking to see if the detective guys have left. They haven't. They're at the end of the driveway in their car. They're probably going to wait there and keep an eye on the place until the cops get here with the warrant. Fortunately for me, I've got two driveways. I might be able to outrun them if I work it right. I stay low in the house, avoid the front windows and door, and quietly gather some things, including my cash stash and a 9mm Glock.

I'm ready to attempt a getaway. I check my watch. 12:20 pm. I look out the laundry room window. The car has gone. Maybe they're hiding further down the road.

There are two ways out of my neighborhood, I just have to pick the right one. I sneak out the door into the garage and open my car door as quietly as possible. I enter, hold my breath, and press the button. The garage door ambles upward noisily, and I have no idea what might be waiting for me on the other side. Finding nothing, I charge down the driveway. I lay it all on the line and take the short route out of the neighborhood, figuring if I can get around them, it's a quicker shot to the freeway, where I can probably lose them, if not their radio.

Miraculously, it appears that no one is waiting for me.

So far, so good.

I try to shake off the lucky feeling, the one that always leads to disaster. I still have to navigate two miles of road before I get to the freeway, the freeway that takes me to Mary's house.

As I'm driving, I think about Rachel's sister, Mary.

As long as I've known her, Mary's been overweight. First time I met her—I'm going back six years now—we'd been talking maybe five minutes when she opened her wallet and carefully removed a clear plastic sheath, out of which she pulled a photo. She glanced at it a few seconds before handing it to me.

"Can you believe this is me?" she said beaming.

At that time, the picture was at least ten years old. It depicted a slim young woman with shoulder-length blond hair and a big smile. She had on a red-and-white tube top that showed a reasonably toned stomach and tan shorts that complimented firm, tapered legs.

"Nice picture," I said at the time.

What I'll never forget is how she took the old photo from my hand as if it were a precious crystal and gave it a long, wistful look before carefully placing it back in the plastic enclosure and ultimately, in her wallet.

I've seen Mary at what, thirty social events since that day? And more times than not, she pulled that old photo out of her wallet and showed it to someone.

I'm planning a quick drive-by. I don't want to enter Mary's house or raise anyone's suspicions; I just want to see if her car is in the driveway. That's where it would be, not in the garage, but in the driveway, or possibly on the street in front of her house. This is because Mary and her husband, Parker, are pack rats. Over the years, they've managed to accumulate so much junk in their garage, there's no room for cars. Now in the neighborhood, I'm a block away. It will be easy to drive past the house and see if her blue 2004 Toyota Celica is there.

It isn't.

My cell phone rings. It's Karen Vogel. I want to confront her but don't know where to begin. I click on the call and hear her screaming before I get the phone to my ear—screaming like she's being attacked.

It takes her a few tries, and her words are interspersed with chokes and sobs, but she finally manages to tell me what's happened. And when I hear it, I'm convinced she knows nothing about Rachel, Mary, or the gangsters.

"Stay on the line," I say. "Don't move. I'm on my way."

I tear down the road to Karen's condo. On the phone, she seems to be hyperventilating. She tells me her cell phone is out of power. She's going to hang up and call me right back on her home phone.

"No!" I say. "Please don't hang up. I'll be there in five minutes."

I hear the click as the phone goes dead. I wait for her to call me back—and wait.

Now I'm pulling into her driveway. I park behind her car. I get out and notice her trunk is shut. I pop it open. It's empty. I look around but see nothing that shouldn't be in her yard. It's the same with the street; everything's normal. I rush to her front door and bang on it while calling her name.

No answer.

I turn the doorknob, and just like in the movies, the door opens. I continue calling Karen's name. I get to the kitchen and see her cell phone on the counter. I check to verify that the battery is dead. It is. On the floor by the back door, I see something that concerns me more than anything else that's happened: Karen's purse. It's lying on the floor open, as if it had fallen or been knocked from the chair. Her wallet and some of the other contents of her purse have spilled out of it and are scattered around the back door.

The back door is open.

Chapter 11

ON THE PHONE moments earlier, Karen had told me she'd come home to change into a suit for her job. She went into her bedroom and changed clothes and then decided she wanted the lipstick she'd left in the purse in her car. She went out to the car, but found no purse. She knew it couldn't be in the trunk, but she opened it anyway.

... And saw the dead body in her trunk.

It was someone she knew, a guy friend—except that her guy friend was an accountant.

Only just now, when she'd seen his blood-soaked body, he was wearing a policeman's uniform.

Like Karen, I was in shock. I listened as she went on and on about how long they'd been friends, how close they were. No, she had no idea how he got into her trunk; she didn't know how long he'd been in there. She'd left the trunk wide open, run straight into her house, and locked the front door. Her first instinct was to call 911, but she was frightened. Since her friend was dressed as a policeman, she was afraid of who might come to her door. Our plan was for me to come here, and together, we'd call 911.

I look around the kitchen for a note or any type of sign she might have left me.

Nothing, unless you count the purse.

I do.

I pick up the items from her purse and place them on her kitchen table. Then I get her purse and dump the contents out on the table.

There's got to be something here.

I pick up the items one by one: a pink leather Coach wallet containing four credit cards, assorted gift cards, a Kentucky driver's license, and fifty-three dollars in cash; a small can of TREsemmé hair spray; a green plastic Clinique compact; sugar-free Tic Tacs, Paradise Mint flavor; an ink pen; an eyebrow pencil; a pack of moistened towelettes; and a checkbook with no entries written in the check ledger. I check the zippered side section and find three packets of Splenda, some loose change, and three cards with romantic messages she'd received with flowers from yours truly.

I open her cell phone again to see if she made any calls after hanging up on me. She did not. I press the redial button on her home phone to see who the last person was that she'd called. The hotel answers.

That's odd. She made the reservations two days ago. There'd be no reason to call today.

I check the digital display for the time of the call: 10:43 am.

Around the time I was running for my life in the park.

Which means someone called her at the hotel from her condo. Someone called to say what? I shake my head to keep myself from imagining all sorts of crazy scenarios. The digital displays on phones, like e-mail time stamps, are notoriously incorrect. She probably called the hotel last night to make sure they charged her for the room. That's the only way they would let her check in at seven this morning, they'd said. The time signature is wrong, that's all.

I can't call the police—they're looking for *me*! You think they'll believe my story? Hell no! They'll show up, check her trunk, find the blood evidence from the "policeman" shot at the park this morning, and I'll be serving twenty to life before you can say, "Dream Team."

The gangster said sometime soon I'll pick up the phone, and he'll be on the line. At the time, I thought he was nuts. Now I'm not so sure. I think he's got Karen, and I'll do whatever I have to in order to get her back safely. I'm thinking he's placed a throwaway cell phone in my home near my computer desk. Maybe I press "one" on the speed dial and he tells me what it will cost to get Karen back safely.

So I'll go home and search for a cell phone. But first, there's something I feel I should do. Since the "policeman" showed up in Karen's trunk, I should check mine for Mary's body. If it's not there, I have another idea where it might be.

I leave Karen's condo and walk slowly to my car. I press the keyless entry for the trunk. It rises to full extension.

It's as empty as Karen's.

So it's on to Plan B: Seneca Park. Since Mary's car wasn't at her house, I figure it must be somewhere around the park. And it's not much of a stretch to assume her body might be in the trunk.

As I open my car door, I get a sudden thought. I retrace my steps to Karen's kitchen and check the digital display on her house phone to see the time of the call I just made to the hotel.

It's accurate.

I stand there, biting my lip, trying to figure out what it means. I retrieve Karen's wallet from her purse, flip it open, and remove her driver's license. I pocket it while walking back to my car, thinking it might come in handy if I decide to involve the cops later on.

In ten minutes, I'm back on Reece Street, two blocks east of the park. I have to be careful since Mary's car won't be the only thing near the scene. Some cops will be there too. They'll have the area cordoned off with yellow crime-scene tape, and I can only hope they'll be too busy collecting evidence to notice me. If someone does recognize me, fine, let them take me. It's only a matter of time before they arrest me anyway, so it's a question of now or later. Normally, I'd say later, but Mary's always been decent to me, so here I am. I happen to know she keeps a key in a small, black magnetic box under her front wheel well. If I can find her car, I should be able to get her trunk open.

I decide to park here, two blocks away, because my car definitely stands out. I find a small opening between two cars and work my way in. I cut the engine, climb out, and within seconds, two young men in their early twenties recognize me. One holds up his hand, gesturing for me to stop. The other is speaking enthusiastically into a walkie-talkie.

Both start moving toward me. I race back to my car and jump in. They're coming from the front, so I have to execute an almost impossible maneuver to get my car out of the space and back out of there before they can stop me. But somehow, I make it, and that lucky feeling sweeps over me. I know it's not much, but at least I'm safe for the moment.

In front of me, the young men are on the street, hands up. No problem, I'll just back up fifty yards and turn down Clifton. I check the rearview mirror and see a black sedan has blocked my escape. The two men I'd seen on my front porch climb out of the car and approach. I look around frantically. The two young men are practically on top of me in the front, the two detectives within ten feet in the back, each coming from opposite ends of the car, tightening the distance like a noose around my neck. There's no way out. It's over. I'm caught.

Chapter 12

"MR. CASE?" SAYS one of the detectives. "My name is Aiden Fry. I'm with VH Productions."

I say nothing, so he adds, "VH Productions, the movie company?"

"I'm sorry—what?"

"We need you to sign a release for the film we shot at the park."

"Film?"

"We just came from your house. I left a business card in your front doorjamb."

"I ... I haven't been home yet," I stutter.

Aiden Fry nods. "We can't guarantee we'll use your reel, but far as I'm concerned, yours was the best performance. By the way," he says, "love your car! Thanks for letting us film it."

I stare at him blankly and then shift my gaze to his partner, then to the walkie-talkie guys, and back to Aiden Fry. "The shooting at the park was part of a movie," I say evenly, trying to see if pronouncing the words makes the idea more plausible.

"A damn good scene," says Aiden Fry's partner.

I think about the people at the park. There must have been eighty of them. Could they have been movie extras? There had been babies— some in strollers, some in blankets— but now that I think about it, something had been missing, something you'd expect to see in this or any other park, even if there had only been a half-dozen people there.

"No dogs at the park this morning," I say.

"Right," the partner says. "Don't like 'em. Too unpredictable. People start chasing you across a field, a dog could spoil the whole shoot."

I nod at him absently, trying to remember the picture I have in my head of Mary being shot. Is it possible the woman I thought was Mary had been an actress who just appeared to be similar? I can't swear I was drugged this morning, but at the time, I had the distinct feeling something had been injected into my neck. The gangster had mentioned Mary just before I exited the limo. Could the drug, in combination with the power of suggestion, cause me to "project" Mary's face onto the actress who had been "shot" during the filming? It seemed so real at the time, but sure, Mary's "wound" could have been faked. She doubled over and fell. Thinking about it now, I don't remember seeing any blood on her. The two joggers shot by Mr. Clean had blood on the backs of their heads, but that could have been placed there before the filming.

That leaves the policeman. His "killing" seems impossible to fake—especially since Karen Vogel saw him in her trunk a few minutes ago, dead.

"The policeman this morning," I say.

"What about him?"

"His head exploded."

Aiden's partner is animated. "Fantastic effect! Incredibly realistic! Wait till you see it on the big screen."

"Uh-huh," I say, watching his face carefully. "How'd you do it?"

"Paintball."

"Someone actually shot him in the head with a paintball?"

"It's a low-velocity gun, and the paintball is twice the normal size, but yeah, it's basically a paintball. With a bunch of plastic goop mixed in."

I think about it that way, but there's something wrong with the explanation.

"I was there. I would have seen a guy shooting a paintball gun."

Aiden Fry says, "The shooter's in the storm drain, ten feet from the cop. He's an expert, but it's still a dicey shot. The guy playing the cop gets fifteen hundred just to take the hit."

"Storm drain's not visible from your angle," Fry's partner adds.

Aiden Fry says, "You want to stay and see the next one?"

"Next one?"

"We shot several today; we've got one more. You can watch if you like. Heck, you can be an extra if you want."

"Extra?" It occurs to me I might be under the influence of some type of psychotropic drug.

"We're shooting the scene one more time. If you want, you can be one of the guys chasing the Schlub back to the limo."

"Schlub?"

He laughs. "Oh, sorry. That's the name of the character in the script, 'Limo Schlub.' Nothing personal."

Chapter 13

I'M NOT BUYING the whole notion that I'd been kidnapped and forced into a movie scene, but I do accept
Aiden Fry's offer to be an extra in the next shoot.

So I'm walking to the park with my new friends when
Fry says, "Oh, the paperwork." He checks his watch. "Any
way you can hang around after the scene?"

He points to the restaurant overlooking the park, the
Rock Creek Diner.

"We can grab a coffee and answer any questions you
have about the release."

I tell him that should work.

He instructs me to join the group on the far side of the
jogging track. I nod and move past cameras and film crew as
they start organizing the extras. While they're being
positioned, I go to the area of Reece Street where Mary and
the policeman had been shot. I stand where they stood, and

sure enough, there's a storm drain nearby. There's a guy with a paintball gun inside, and he motions me to move along. I turn and see two actors approaching. One appears to be Karen's friend, the "policeman" I'd seen this morning getting his head blown off. The other is my sister-in-law Mary, or her identical twin. I wave; the lady smiles and waves back. It's not Mary, but the resemblance is remarkable.

The "policeman" isn't as friendly. He gives me a bored look and continues staring at me as if trying to place me from somewhere. I wave my hands at him like I'd done earlier this morning, when I thought he was a real cop. He makes the connection and shouts, "Get him!" and laughs.

"That's me," I say. "Limo Schlub."

It's clear someone is royally fucking with me because these are definitely the people I saw this morning. But are they fucking with Karen too? Did they use a body double of her "policeman" friend to spook Karen? If this guy is her close friend, why would he allow it? And why have I automatically assumed Karen's been kidnapped? Maybe she heard a noise before I got there and ran to a neighbor's house. She might be back at her condo by now.

Of course, if she were home, she'd have called me by now.

I don't have time to think about it because the scene has started. It plays out exactly the same way mine did, except the "Schlub" looks nothing like me, the limo is different, Mr. Clean is different, and the car that peels out after the two shots are fired is not a red Audi R8, but a tricked-out Camaro.

When the Schlub starts running back to the limo, I start backing up, out of the scene. I keep a close eye on "Mary" and the "policeman," who continue to lie where they were "shot." I back up across the track, and ... shit! I trip over a picnic basket and fall to the ground. I get up, embarrassed, hoping I didn't get caught on film and realize there's no one watching me. I'm well out of the scene. I'm on Reece Street now, half a block west of "Mary" and the "policeman," and they're still down. I duck behind a pickup truck, sit on one knee, and watch them.

Two minutes go by, and finally, a camera truck drives to the corner where the Camaro had been parked. Some cameramen get out and start fiddling around with equip-ment, and I can see they're about to start filming from that angle. I'm on the street side of the truck, which means I'll be part of the film unless I move. I stay low and scoot behind the pickup as a group of "policemen" rush to the "crime scene" to tend to "Mary" and the "policeman." They're on police radios, barking out codes, with guns drawn, looking very "movie-ish." A moment later, an ambulance roars up behind me, continues past my position, and comes to a stop beside the victims.

The EMS guys jump out of the ambulance and get to work. They put "Mary" on a stretcher and load her into the ambulance. As for the "policeman," they shake their heads. The cops start overacting to the point I'm certain this scene will be scrapped during the first edit.

Now I'm completely convinced the movie scene is genuine, and I was kidnapped and forced to be in it. Someone placed a Mary look-alike in the cast so I would witness her pretend murder. They also inserted a body double of Karen's friend into the scene, and maybe these are the warnings I should be concentrating on instead of the "K" and "V."

I watch the EMS guys climb back into the ambulance, put it in gear, and roar past me. I turn my head to watch and see them fly past a line of parked cars that includes a blue 2004 Toyota Celica—like Mary drives.

I stay put until I hear the director yell, "Cut!" Then I get up and start walking toward Mary's car. Two coeds are rushing toward me, curious about what's going on in the park behind me. As they approach, one says, "Any big-time movie stars here?"

"None that I recognized," I say.

"Told you!" she says to her friend. To me, she says, "Have a nice day," and they hurry past me toward the film crew. I suppose for Louisville, this is a major event despite the lack of big-time movie stars.

Looking through the windows, I'm positive this is Mary's car because of all the junk inside. I now know that Mary wasn't in the film, so why is her car here? I look around to make sure no one's watching me as I reach up into the wheel well, feel around a bit, and finally extract the magnetic key box. I retrieve the key, slide it into the door lock, and enter the car. I'm in no rush to check the trunk. I'm hoping to find some evidence that she's *not* in the trunk.

I'm sitting in the driver's seat, looking around. Mary's car is as messy as her garage. There are papers and envelopes and fast-food wrappers all over the seats and floor. It would take an hour to sift through all this crap, and anyway, I doubt there's anything here that will help make sense of the last few hours.

So the car looks like Mary's, and it had a key in the wheel well like Mary's. I open the glove box, and the insurance registration confirms what had seemed so obvious: it's definitely my sister-in-law's car.

So where's Mary, in the trunk? I laugh at the thought.

I shuffle a few items around but can't find her purse, which means she's probably having lunch at the Rock Creek Diner.

I wonder if Mary came to see the film shoot this morning because someone told her the actress filming the scene could be her twin. Or maybe she was never here at all this morning. Maybe she showed up for this final shoot because someone called and told her she looked like the actress who'd been at Seneca Park all morning. She might have only been here a half hour or so. Maybe she was one of the park extras just now, one of the people chasing "Limo Schlub!"

I'm feeling much better about the day. Sure, the whole gangster thing was nutty, but they were obviously actors. I'm not as happy about the trick someone played on me with Rachel and the bra thing. Someone obviously found out about my tryst with Karen this morning and wanted to make me squirm. And they're making Karen squirm about it too, by subjecting her to a fake body.

Maybe that's why Karen disappeared. Maybe the warning worked, and she wants nothing to do with me now.

I'm not happy one of the actors rendered me unconscious and stole my car this morning, but it all fits in with the theme. I just have to rack my brain and try to figure out who has the motive and means to fuck with me like this.

On the bright side, it turns out Rachel's okay. No one molested her or tied her up. Someone did pretend to be her and ruined one of her bras trying to make some sort of sick point about my affair, but it's clear that Rachel doesn't know about Karen—not yet, anyway. And as far as I can tell, Mary's safe.

Look in the trunk!

I get out my cell phone and call Karen's home phone. It rings eight times, and I hang up. I'm sure she's fine, but I'm worried she might be planning to end things without ever speaking to me again. If so, I've got an ace in the hole: her driver's license. I might be able to parlay that into a discussion about getting back together.

What about her purse? What woman would go off and leave her purse and wallet lying on the floor?

I can only think of two scenarios that ring true: either she's been kidnapped or she's part of the hoax.

Part of the hoax? Doubtful. She was too frightened. No one could act it out that convincingly. Her screams were sincere. Maybe the guy in her trunk wasn't her friend, maybe he wasn't dead, but she was definitely convinced. And she's gone, at least for now.

I exit the car and look up and down the street. On the far side of the park, away from me, the film crew and most of the extras are still hanging around. On this end, still a distance from me, people are walking their dogs, flinging Frisbees, and jogging down side streets. I pull out my cell phone and dial Karen's number again.

I try to remember her office number, but can't quite conjure it. I give up, dial information, and have the operator put me through. I've spoken to Dana, the receptionist, before. She answers, and I tell her it's me.

Dana says, "Hi, Sam, Karen's not here yet. Would you like to leave a message on her voice mail?"

"No, that's all right," I say. There's a long pause before I realize I'm still on the line.

Dana notices too and says, "Karen called in sick this morning, but she called back at—" She pauses. I hear paper rustling. Dana's found her notes. "Karen called at eleven fifteen to say she was feeling better, said she'd be here after lunch."

I check my watch. It's nearly one thirty. "You haven't heard from her since?"

"Not a word," Dana says. "You think something's wrong?"

I think something's definitely wrong!

"No," I say. "She probably had a recurrence. I'm sure we'll both hear from her soon."

"If she calls or comes in, I'll have her call you," she says.

"Thanks, Dana."

I end the call and try Karen's home phone again and her cell phone, for good measure. Her cell phone prompts a factory-installed voice message: "The cellular customer you're calling is out of range or out of service at this time. Please hang up and try your call again."

I end the call and look around the area again but still don't see Mary. I don't want to hang around waiting for her. I want to go home and see if I can find a throwaway phone.

I'm sure Mary's okay, and anyway, if she were to show up, what on earth would I say to her?

Hi, Mary, I thought you'd been killed this morning, so I'm snooping through your car looking for evidence of your death. Oh, and also, I'm wondering if you know anything about my affair with Karen Vogel or if you know who might have kidnapped me this morning, put me in a movie scene, stole my car, wrote some initials on your sister's bra, and placed it in my laundry hamper, and—oh yeah, while we're on the subject—do you know anyone who looks just like Rachel that might want to be tied up to the floor of our kitchen and photographed seminude?

I place Mary's spare key back into the magnetic key box. I'm about to place it into the wheel well when the voice in my head screams, *Check the trunk!*

I slide the little key box open for the second time, take out the key, place it in the trunk lock, and turn till it clicks. I can't say if the car has been in the sun for hours like I originally thought, but the metal is hot against my fingertips as I slowly lift the lid of the trunk.

Though widely considered a sports car, the 2004 Toyota Celica has an astonishing amount of trunk space. Mary's two-door, four-seat model contains seventeen cubic feet of cargo space. Enough volume, it turns out, to hold my sister-in-law's dead body.

Chapter 14

I'M GROUNDED, BUT the world around me starts swirling at an insane speed, like I'm stuck in the eye of a tornado, only there's no flying cow. I want to vomit. I want to fall to the ground and pound my fists and scream until this crazy day ends. But I don't do any of those things. I don't do them because—all the madness notwithstanding—I seem to have gained enough clarity of focus to consider that three hours ago, I'd been completely fooled by a photograph of someone I thought was my own wife. So, although this definitely appears to be a dead body, it's within the realm of possibility that the woman in the trunk isn't dead or if she is, she might not be Mary.

Keeping my head above the trunk, I reach my hand in and poke her body with my finger. If she's faking, she's good. I feel around wondering if what I'm about to do will keep me out of heaven. I do it anyway. I poke and prod the body until I find one of her boobs. I pinch it as hard as I can between my thumb and forefinger until I know the woman in Mary's trunk is not pretending to be dead.

I understand on a gut level I have to do something right now that I don't want to do. I have to make absolutely certain it's her. I duck my head a few inches into the trunk, and I'm suddenly aware of the searing stench. It fills my nostrils, burns my eyes, and triggers my gag reflex. I feel the bile working its way up my throat, and I start dry-heaving. I'm forced to turn my head away. I put my hands on my knees and assume the classic vomit stance. Then it dawns on me I'm standing on a public street with my back to a wide-open trunk that contains the body of a dead woman. I spin around, lower the trunk most of the way, and look around carefully to see if anyone is watching me.

I see no one but the dead lady in the trunk and a bunch of people in the park who are busy doing their own thing.

I take a deep breath, lift the trunk a couple of feet, and focus on the woman's face. I'm certain it's Mary, but the photograph they gave me of Rachel fooled me, so again, I have to be sure. Fortunately, I know a way to positively identify Rachel's sister.

Last year, Mary and Parker had the family over for their tenth anniversary. The girls and their mom were giggling over something that turned out to be scandalous by their standards: Mary had gotten a tattoo. Of course, after hearing the explanation, it turned out to be more charming than titillating. She and Parker had gotten each other's names tattooed on their ring fingers to celebrate the occasion.

"Hurt like hell!" Mary said at the time.

The lady in the trunk is wearing a wedding band that looks exactly like Mary's. I take another deep breath, prop the trunk open with my left hand, reach into the trunk with my right, and tug on the woman's wedding ring until I see the tattoo under it that says, "Parker."

Mary's dead.

I slam the trunk shut so hard that something breaks and it springs back open slightly. I fall on it, face first. My hands begin shaking uncontrollably. I press them against the hot metal to hold them still. The heat from the metal burns my forehead. I can feel my heart beating in my ears. I try to stand and feel my knees buckle. My stomach lurches, and this time, I can't hold it back. I vomit hard on the street behind Mary's car.

Then something hits Mary's back window just above my head, and an explosion of glass slams into the back of her car, followed by the sound of a gunshot and then another and another! I look up and see four men—not policemen, not actors, not gangsters, but midgets, four of them— running toward me with guns drawn, firing.

Chapter 15

HOLY SHIT!

I run to the driver's side, fumble in my pocket for the key, and—bam!—Mary's backseat window, street-side, sends a shower of glass fragments raining through the cabin. Shards of glass are everywhere, including the back of my right ear and neck. I force the car onto the street, smashing the rear of the car parked in front of me. I'm pedal to the metal, but Mary's Celica is a far cry from my Audi. Still, I'm barreling down Reece, toward the camera truck and puzzled crew and cast members who are trying to jump out of my way. I brake hard to keep from hitting someone. Several shots ring out in unison and hit something metal behind me, making a rat-a-tat machine-gun sound. I glance at the rearview mirror and can't see anything behind me. Another rat-a-tat sound makes me aware I owe my life to having broken the trunk latch moments ago. It had risen up and caught the bullets that were meant to strike the back of my head. Feeling lucky again, I lurch forward and put Seneca Park behind me.

I'm racing down Reece in a Celica with Mary's dead body in the trunk—the wide-open trunk! I don't want to get stuck like this at a busy traffic intersection, so I slow down, take a side street for a block, turn right again, and head back toward the park.

No one on earth expects me to do this, right?

I stop and park a couple of cars away from the corner of Cannons Lane and Rock Creek, not far from where the gangsters parked their limo this morning. I take off my left shoe and sock, place the sock on my right hand, and begin wiping down every surface I might have touched in the front seat. I get out of the car and do the same there, wiping down everything including the wheel well, roof, and top of the trunk. I even wipe down Mary's ring before lowering the broken trunk.

I hear some animated elfin chatter up ahead and see the four midgets—the ones who'd shot at me moments earlier— thirty yards away, laughing and high-fiving each other before climbing into a waiting limousine and driving off.

What the hell is that all about?

I'd understand if they'd hit me or killed me or stopped me. But they'd only succeeded in scaring me off. *Is that what they're celebrating? And if so,* I wonder, *why?* I think about following them in Mary's car, but I decide it's more important to check on Karen.

I put my sock and shoe back on and walk the two blocks back and one block over to my Audi. No one's blocking me this time. I climb in, back the car out, and start driving to Karen Vogel's condo.

A shrill noise explodes from under the driver's seat, and I'm so startled I nearly crash the car.

It's a cell phone—not my cell phone, mind you, but a new one that's hidden under the driver's seat, the same place they'd hidden the photo of Rachel this morning. Only it's the loudest cell phone ever built. It could wake the dead.

I click the "talk" button. It's the gangster.

"We got your lady with us," he says.

They've kidnapped Karen!

"You'll never believe where we found her. Hey, she seems upset. She doesn't want me to tell you where we found her. Funny, huh?"

"Leave her out of this!" I scream. "What the fuck's going on here? What do you want from me?"

"You like, you can talk to her now. But only for a second."

I hear a muffled sound as the phone is being passed, and then a voice shouts, "Sam! Oh my God, these men—"

I feel like I'm on a hundred-mile-an-hour roller coaster to hell, with Stephen King at the controls.

The voice isn't Karen's.

Then I hear a scream.

... not Karen Vogel's scream ...

Rachel's.

The voice and scream are Rachel's. They've kidnapped—are kidnapping—my wife.

"Oh God! Please!" I shout. "Let her go. I'll do anything. I swear to God, *anything*. Just let her go!"

"Sam, you sound like you're ready to talk. So what I want, you go home now, go home, get on your ... whatcha call ... Web site, wait for my call."

"Look," I tell him, "let Rachel go, you don't need her. If this is about the money, I'll do whatever you want. I'll give you the codes. I'll give them to you right now. Just let her go."

"You got the codes memorized?"

"I do."

"All of them?"

"All of them."

There was a pause on the other end of the line while he thought about it. Finally, he says, "Go home, Sam. We'll call you soon."

I hear the sound of Rachel struggling in the background. "Rachel!" I yell.

Then I hear a couple of sharp sounds, and Rachel emits a bloodcurdling scream that sickens me to the core. I'm trembling with fury and helplessness, thinking about that Mr. Clean motherfucker putting his hands on my wife. "Rachel!" I yell again but realize I'm speaking into a dead connection.

Chapter 16

I FEEL TRAPPED, like a rabbit caught in a snare. Would I give up the codes to the fortunes of the world's most dangerous men in order to save Rachel? Of course I would, the same way a rabbit would chew off its own leg to get away.

Because this shit has got to stop.

I'm on Westport Road, heading home, wondering if the gangster and Mr. Clean are there with Rachel. He seemed taken with the idea of where they found her, so my best guess is she was on her way home. Last we'd talked, she was heading to lunch. I'd mentioned I was at the house, and I probably sounded funny to her. She asked if I was sick, so maybe she decided to come home and check on me and got ambushed.

I realize there's another possibility. Maybe she knows about Karen. Maybe she went to Karen's condo during her lunch hour. Maybe the gangster picked her up at Karen's.

Did he pick up Karen too?

No. He would have said. Or Rachel would have said something about her just now.

So where's Karen Vogel? And why was her purse upended on the kitchen floor?

I want to check on Karen, but I have to get home in order to save Rachel. I've known Karen one month, had sex with her exactly once, and my life has turned into a living hell. Mary's dead, Rachel's been kidnapped, and God only knows what's going on with Karen.

I want to pick up speed and get home as quickly as possible, but the road has tapered into two lanes and I'm behind a line of cars. We're moving, but regular speed. There's nothing to do but follow the other cars past the church, soccer field, assorted fast-food restaurants, and ...

My cell phone rings—mine, not the new one. I pick up.

"You trying to rob me, Sam?"

"Who is this?"

"Donovan Creed."

Shit!

"No, sir, of course not." My mind is racing. Creed is the professional hit man, the last guy on the list I'd want to piss off. Why on earth would he think I'm trying to—*Wait, the computer!* I'd entered Creed's code a couple hours ago when I thought Rachel might have been kidnapped, before I found out she was okay. Though now she's been kidnapped for real. *Christ, will you just listen to me? Can this really be happening? It must be.* You simply can't make this shit up.

Creed is waiting for me to say something, but I'm trying to figure out how he knew I'd entered his code into my computer. Finally, he speaks.

"Sam, you must be in a lot of trouble."

"Why do you say that?"

"Sam, listen to me. Whatever you think your problems are, they're nothing compared to dealing with me."

Creed has this eerie kind of voice. Just hearing him say my name sends a chill down my spine. He's right; I don't want to have to deal with him. I decide to come clean.

"They've kidnapped my wife."

"Rachel."

How the fuck does everyone know Rachel's name?

"They're hurting her," I say. "She's my *wife*. What would you do if you were me?"

"If I were you?" he says. "If I were you, I wouldn't fuck with Donovan Creed."

"What, you're saying you'd let your own wife die?"

"This discussion is going nowhere," he says.

"No," I say, emboldened. "I want to know what you'd do in my place."

"Sam, we had this discussion two years ago, when I asked if I could trust you with my money."

I think about that, but the other thing is weighing on my mind— not Rachel, God help me, but the other thing. I can't help it. That's how my brain is wired. I have to ask him.

"Mr. Creed, how did you know?"

"About the code being entered? I had a frequency chip imbedded into my hip."

"You what?"

"It's tuned to the frequency of the digits."

I'm stuck at a traffic light, wondering if I should run it. Better not. I don't need cops on my ass. "The sixteen digits have a frequency?"

"Sam, you've got your specialty, but this part is way over your head. Let me put it this way: You put together a nice little money-moving scheme. It's off the government's radar. You tell me you can be trusted. I'm in. So I get my people to put together a little device that starts vibrating the minute you—or someone else—enters the code on your computer."

"What's the range of this device?" I say.

"The planet Earth."

The light turns green. Something else suddenly comes to mind. "Wait a minute. The computer I used today—it's new. Your device can't be keyed to this one."

Creed sighs. "Sam, I'm quite familiar with your computer."

"How's that possible?"

I've been living in your house for two years."

"What?"

"You control a quarter billion dollars of my money. Do I really strike you as a hands-off type of guy?"

No. You strike me as an insane type of guy!

I turn on Frey's Hill and circle Sawyer Park. I'm almost home.

"Where are you?" I say, wondering if he might be waiting for me at my house.

"Sam, we're running out of time, so don't interrupt. I know you're almost home. I know this because someone's placed a device on your car. I'm tuned to it now, just as they are. You and I need to make a pact. You're going to do whatever I say, no matter how crazy it sounds, and I'll come get you. I'll save you, Sam. Provided you agree not to rip me off."

"You'll come get me? You mean you're coming to my house?"

Creed sighs. "No, Sam, I mean, when they take you away, I'll find you and save you, provided you refuse to give them my code."

"What about Rachel?" I say.

He pauses. "Sam, when it all goes down, if that's what you want, I'll save Rachel too."

I wonder what the hell that means, but before I can ask, he says, "Did they give you a phone?"

"Yes."

"Okay. They'll expect you to go straight to your computer, but instead, you're going to go down the first set of stairs to the basement. Then you're going to run the length of the basement up the spiral staircase all the way to the top. Then you're going to hide in the secret room you built for the little girl you never had."

"How did you know about—"

"Sam, you're in this deeper than you think, so do what I say. You're going to take their phone with you. They'll keep calling you, and at some point, they'll force you to answer it. They're going to want the codes. You're going to refuse."

"What if I give them just one code? Not yours, but someone big. You think the gangster would set Rachel free?"

"He doesn't have Rachel."

"But I heard—"

"What you heard was a tape of Rachel. He put the recorder up to the phone to make you think he had her."

"How do you *know* that?"

"It's my job to know."

"Fine," I say. "So where's Rachel?"

"That I don't know. Not yet, anyway. But they'll be taking you to wherever she is. And I'll be following."

"If the gangster doesn't have her, who does?"

"I'm not sure yet. But I'll help you get her back, if that's what you both want."

"Why do you keep saying it that way? Of course it's what we want!"

"Then do exactly what I tell you, and don't question or second-guess me."

"Fine."

"Sam, why did you stop just now? Turn in your driveway. They're coming."

"I was just checking the yard."

"Get in the house, now! Go to the secret room. I'll get you through this." He pauses and then says, "If what?"

I think a second. "If I don't let them steal your money."

The line goes dead. I click the button to open the garage door.

Chapter 17

I SHUT OFF the engine and rush into the house and down the steps like Creed told me. Then I run down the long, dark basement hallway at full speed. Before I hit the spiral staircase, the cell phone in my hand starts blaring like a weather siren. I could be shouting my location through a bullhorn, and it wouldn't lead them to me any faster. I stop where I am and turn on a hallway light. I try to find the mute button. Suddenly, the driveway sensors are going crazy. The cell phone is still blaring, and I've got to find a way to mute it and set it to vibrate only. I fumble with it some more, but it's not my phone, and I'm having trouble with it, and ...

Shit!

I drop it on the floor. I hear men's voices shouting at the front door one floor up.

This fucking cell phone is ringing so loudly I fear for my eardrums.

There's a heavy banging sound above me as they try to smash through the front door. These are four-inch solid mahogany doors. If I were them, I'd try an easier entry point.

There! I finally get the cell-from-hell phone muted. I run to the spiral staircase and take the steps two at a time. There are thirty-eight steps in all from the basement to the top landing, and I'm only halfway up when I hear the glass in the back door shatter. Within seconds, they're swarming the kitchen, and I've still got a dozen steps to go.

I hug the wall and continue climbing. When I reach the top, I tread softly because they're in the hall below me, heading to my study. I enter the room we built for the daughter we never had. I leave both doors open—the bedroom and closet doors—so it won't be obvious I'm in here. I creep to the bookcase and pull on one of the shelves, and the bookcase door opens. I flip on the interior light switch and nearly have a heart attack.

Donovan Creed is in there, holding his finger to his lips. He hands me a small bottle of water and a piece of metal in the shape of a pill.

"Swallow this," he whispers.

I start to protest, and his hand becomes a blur. Suddenly, he's holding a knife to my throat.

"It's a transmitter," he whispers. "If you shit it out before I find you, swallow it again."

"That's disgusting!" I whisper.

"So's dying."

I swallow the pill and think about how normal my life had been just yesterday. Creed motions me to get in the secret room and close the bookcase door. He turns his back to me and opens the attic access door. I haven't been in the secret room since I can remember, but I do remember there wasn't an access door when we built the house.

The phone buzzes softly in my pocket. I put my hand on Creed's shoulder and whisper, "Let me in there with you."

He shakes his head. "No. They need to find and capture you. Otherwise, we'll never find Rachel."

I hear men running through the house shouting my name. They're all over the place, but they're concentrating on the main floor and basement for now. In a matter of moments, they'll be charging up the steps. Creed ducks his head and enters the attic. He stops, and holding the door open, whispers, "They'll probably take you somewhere and force you to enter the codes. Your job is to stall them till I get there."

I hear shouting at the base of the steps. I pull the bookcase door shut. There's no lock on it because Rachel read somewhere that once upon a time, a kid got locked in her secret room, fell asleep, and got strangled in her blanket. But I doubt anyone is going to find me in here because on the closet side, the bookcase is filled with children's books, and there's no reason anyone would think it leads to a secret room.

I whisper, "What if they force me to give the codes before you get to me?"

"Resist as long as you can," he says.

I hear what sounds like at least a dozen men rushing up the stairs, shouting orders to each other. They're coming for me. They're practically on top of me.

"That's it?" I whisper fiercely. "That's all you've got? Hold out as long as I can?"

"There's this," he says. "If you're forced to enter the codes, enter mine last. Say it."

"I'll enter your code last."

"No matter what," he says.

"No matter what."

With that, he shuts the attic door. I hear a soft click and wonder how he had time to build the door and install a lock. Then I remember how he said he'd lived in my house for two years.

Chapter 18

I HEAR A dozen different voices, all angry and frustrated. Someone has a walkie-talkie in the upstairs hallway on the opposite side of the secret room wall. I hear him asking one person after another if they've found me. Then he sounds like he's on the phone. I can't hear what he's saying, but a moment later, he shouts, "Ted! Hook up a wire to the speaker system. I want Sam to hear this."

Ten minutes later, a man's voice—not the gangster's—is coming through my in-home stereo system.

"Sam," he says, "we've never met, but I know you can hear me. I'll give you thirty seconds to come out of your hiding place with your hands in the air."

For the next thirty seconds, the cell phone in my pocket vibrates softly.

Then the man says, "Sam, I have Rachel here with me."

Bullshit! I think. *It's a tape.*

"I'm going to have a little chat with your wife, and you can listen in." There's a short pause, and then he says, "Rachel, I've got Sam on the phone. I told him you're with me, but I don't think he believes me. Tell him what time it is."

In a small, frightened voice, Rachel says, "It's ten till three."

"You hear that, Sam? Check your watch."

I do. And it is ten till three. Still, he could have prerecorded this on a tape and waited until now to play it. I'm not sure I believe their timing could be that good, but I'm not ready to surrender yet; I need more proof.

"Sam, I'm usually a patient man. Everyone says that about me. I had this whole thing worked out. It was incredibly elaborate. But you screwed up my timetable when you saw that situation in the trunk at the park a little while ago. I won't give Rachel the details just yet. I'm not a monster after all." He chuckles. "Well, some say I am."

The phone in my pocket vibrates again.

"Answer the phone, Sam," he says. "Now!"

Go fuck yourself! I say to him, in my head. Another half minute passes, but I still don't answer the phone.

"Sam, for the next thirty seconds, I'm not going to call you. I'll be too busy beating your wife."

Ten seconds later, Rachel's screams are playing throughout my house. She's being tortured. I try to drown out her shrieks by focusing on what Creed told me, to hold out as long as possible. I wonder what he could be doing in the attic to help me. Does he have someone on the outside, triangulating the cell signal? Rachel's screams die down. I hear her whimpering.

"Sam, you're a stronger man than I am," the voice says. "If this were my wife, I'd be dying inside. Perhaps when this is all over, you'll want to reevaluate your relationship."

The phone buzzes in my pocket. I ignore it.

"Very well, Sam. It's only going to get worse." I hear him sigh, which means everyone in my house hears it too. "Rachel," he says, "take off your clothes."

"No," she says. "Please."

My fists clench so tightly it feels like my knucklebones are going to burst through the skin. I shut my eyes and wince.

I hear him slap her. She cries out in agony. "That's right," he says. "Start with the blouse ... good girl. Okay, now the skirt ..."

I shift my weight from my right foot to my left and back to my right. I feel like throwing myself through the wall. I've got to give Creed as much time as possible to do whatever it is he's trying to do. But I don't want this man to hurt my wife.

"Now the bra ..."

"Please," she says.

He hits her again. But this time, it's not a slap. I think he punched her. It sounds as though she slammed into something and crumbled to the floor. Maybe I'm reading that into whatever happened, imagining the worst, but I'm not imagining her sobs. I hear her whimper, "Please. Don't hit me again. I'll do it. I'll do whatever you want."

The man's voice says, "You hear that, Sam? Okay then, Rachel, show me the rest."

My heart is in my throat. My breath is coming out in short gasps, like a pregnant woman giving a Lamaze birth. Just when I think I'll get through this part, I hear Rachel's voice say, "Sam ... I'm so sorry."

It's more than I can bear. The cell phone vibrates in my pocket again, and I answer.

"Where are you, Sam?" the man asks.

"In the upstairs closet," I say. "Please. Stop hurting Rachel. Tell your men not to shoot. I'm coming out."

Thirty seconds of silence pass before he comes back on the line. "Okay, Sam, come on out. They won't hurt you."

"Where's Rachel?"

"We'll take you to her."

"Promise you'll leave her alone?"

"I'll promise nothing. But if you cooperate, it'll go easier for her."

I push the bookcase open and exit the closet; eight men are standing in a semicircle, pointing rifles at me. I don't know much about guns, so I can't give you the makes, model numbers, calibers, or whatever. I can tell you that all the rifles are equipped with silencers, but that's about it.

Someone orders me to get facedown on the floor with my hands behind my back. I do what they say, and someone else ties a couple of pieces of plastic around my wrists. Then that person—or someone else—plunges a hypodermic needle into my neck.

Chapter 19

I DON'T KNOW where I am.

I'm lying on my back on a hard surface, and it's so dark I can't see my hand moving in front of my face. I lift my head slightly and try to look around, but I get nothing, like I'm caught in a black hole.

How can anything be this dark?

I have a strong sense of breathing stale air, like maybe I'm in some type of enclosure.

Where's Rachel?

I shout, "Rachel!" and listen to the sound my voice makes. It's muffled, but not extremely so, which tells me at least I'm not in a coffin. I'm in an enclosure of some sort, but thank God it's not a coffin.

Where's Rachel?

I call her name again but get no response. I raise my arms up, like I'm doing a bench press, and get nothing but air, so I figure there's probably enough height to sit up. I jerk myself up to a sitting position and raise my arms high above my head. There seems to be plenty of height, so maybe I'm not in an enclosure, though possibly a small room of some sort.

My inner voice says, *How long have we been unconscious?*

I have no way to tell. It's too dark to see my watch. Hell, we—I could have been here an hour, a day, a week ...

No. Not a week. Not even a day. I would have had to pee by now.

If I'd peed in here, surely I'd be able to tell. I sniff the air and touch my clothing. No, I haven't peed. So I'm guessing I've been unconscious a couple of hours—however long it took them to carry me out of my house and transport me to wherever I am.

I slowly attempt to stand. My legs are wobbly, but I manage to get to my feet. I reach up until I touch a smooth surface, which I estimate at about seven feet high. I put my arms in front of me and take a few tentative steps before touching a glass wall. I follow it sideways a few steps until I feel the intersection of another glass wall. I follow the sur-face the entire length of the rectangle and realize I'm in a glass cage, approximately eight feet wide and fourteen feet long. I wonder if Rachel is in a similar cage. Wherever she is, she doesn't deserve this shit.

Suddenly, a light comes on and then more lights. Lots of incredibly bright lights are coming on above and around me in all directions. The sudden brightness is too much for my eyes. Though I'm desperate to see what's happening, I have to shield my eyes for more than a minute before they can adjust. While I manage a few short peeks, all I gain is watery eyes and only the blurriest information.

I allow enough time for my vision to acclimate. I blink a couple of times to finally bring the world around me into focus. I wipe the remaining tears from my eyes with the tail of my shirt and see that the walls of my cage are not made of glass, but rather a thick slab of Lucite. Beyond the walls that hold me captive, I see that my Lucite enclosure sits in the middle of a huge, empty room that looks like an indoor parking lot. The bottom of my enclosure is made of wood and metal and is elevated several feet above the parking lot's concrete floor. I try to see what's holding up my cage, but I can't find any angle that allows me to glimpse the structure beneath me. But wait, I turn to one side and look through the clear material. I see something that takes me by surprise: the giant cab of a truck, the kind of cab used to haul large flatbed trucks across the country.

My Lucite container is attached to one ... only, in this case, I'm the cargo.

I turn my attention to the area inside my cage and find a camper toilet, an insulated cooler, a blanket, and a pillow. There's one more item, located on top of the cooler: a laptop computer.

I appear to be alone in this giant underground parking lot. I'm assuming "underground," because there are no windows and no natural light, and moments ago, the room was so dark it seems impossible it could be located above ground.

My inner voice says, *How long have we been stuck here, Sam?*

I look at my watch: April 22, 2009.

That doesn't make sense.

It was April 12 a few hours ago.

There's no way I've been here ten days!

But what if you have? My inner voice says. Not in this cage, maybe, but what if they put you in a room somewhere to monitor you?

"Monitor me for what?" I ask myself.

What if they were waiting for you to shit out the monitoring device you swallowed? Maybe they kept you sedated somewhere all this time, and when you finally gave up the device, they brought you here.

"No," I tell myself. "Wherever they would have put me, Creed would have found me in less than ten days. I'm still holding the device. He's coming for me. He'll get us out of here."

I look at my watch again. Three hours have passed, and it's now April 2, 2008. I watch the hours, minutes, and calendar going forward and backward randomly through time. Every few seconds, my watch resets to a different date and time, none of which hold any significance that I can determine.

I shout, "You people are nuts! Just tell me what you want and let us go!"

Across the parking lot, I see a huge garage-type door start to rise. When it gets to full height, the cab of a large truck enters. As it continues through the door, I can see that the bed of the truck is made of Lucite and has the same dimensions as my cage, which confirms everything I suspect about what's beneath my cage.

I'm trapped in a Lucite container attached to a flatbed truck.

The other truck pulls up alongside mine and stops maybe twelve feet away. The windows and windshield of the truck's cab are mirrored, so there's no way to tell who's driving it. I concentrate on the part I can see. I'm staring at a Lucite cage just like mine, equipped just like mine, except that it has no laptop that I can see. In the cage across from me, the blanket is covering what appears to be a body. I bang my fist against the transparent wall that holds me captive and shout, "Rachel!"

I bang the Lucite wall again and continue to shout her name, but I already know these units are completely soundproofed because the huge truck across from me entered the room and stopped a few feet away from me and I never heard the slightest sound as it did so.

I scream my wife's name again and again. I kick the wall in frustration. I pick up the cooler and smash it against the wall, but it rebounds like a rubber hammer hitting a concrete wall. Several water bottles and wrapped sandwiches fly out and scatter across the floor of my cage. I stand with my palms pressed against the Lucite wall and stare at the motionless form under the blanket for what seems like an hour.

Could they have killed her? Beaten her to death? Have I lost the love of my life because of a stupid computer program?

Then I think I see the slightest movement. Are my eyes playing a trick on me? No—there it is again. She's alive! Thank God! It's destroying me to think about seeing Rachel like this, but I need to see her, need to reassure her, need to let her know how sorry I am to have caused all this to happen.

The blanket finally pushes away, and I can see it's not Rachel who's trapped in the cage twelve feet away from me.

My heart sinks.

It's Donovan Creed.

Chapter 20

A VOICE COMES through a hidden speaker in the floor of my cubicle.

"Mr. Case, I believe you already know the man in the unit before you. His name is Donovan Creed. Mr. Creed is a former CIA assassin and currently works for the Department of Homeland Security as a clandestine terrorist assassin. He tests crowd control weapons for the United States Army and performs freelance contract killing for various people, including a regional underworld crime boss."

The voice goes silent. I look at Creed hopefully, but he's offering no expression to encourage me. I wonder if his cubical is getting the sound. I turn my palms upward in the universal gesture, "What's going on?"

Creed shrugs.

"That's it?" I scream. "You *promised* me! I was *counting* on you! You were my only hope!"

Creed appears disinterested. He looks away, walks over to his toilet, and starts peeing.

The voice in my cubicle says, "Mr. Case—may I call you, Sam?" The voice pauses a moment and then continues, "There will be no rescue, Sam, not until you give us the codes. You do this by powering up your laptop and entering them. You can start with Mr. Creed's." The voice pauses again and then says, "Don't waste your time trying to access the Internet to attempt a rescue. Your computer is not equipped for online access."

When Creed finishes peeing, I start pounding my hands on the wall of my cell to get his attention. I hurl a number of curses at him for good measure, but he appears completely oblivious to the commotion I'm making. Instead, he goes to the far corner of his cell and presses his hands against the Lucite edges. He works his hands up and down the clear material, staring intently at the intersections of Lucite, as if trying to see what he's gotten himself into and how he might possibly get out.

"It's useless!" I shout.

The voice comes back on. "You're right, Sam; it *is* useless. But don't fault Mr. Creed. He's not accustomed to being helpless. Nor is he likely to accept his plight quickly. You, on the other hand, are fortunate. You have something we want. Creed's going to die in his cell eventually, but you can leave whenever you wish. All you have to do is enter the codes."

"So ... you can hear me?" I say.

"We can hear you."

"Where's Rachel?"

"Somewhere safe," the voice says. "And she'll continue to be safe as long as you cooperate."

"I want to see her."

"You're in no position to make demands, Sam. However, if you're willing to give us Mr. Creed's code, we'll arrange for you to see her briefly."

"I don't know Creed's code or any of the others."

"You told our associate you had them memorized."

"I lied. But if you can get me my personal computer, I might be able to access the data file—"

"Not going to happen, Sam."

"I might be able to reproduce them," I say, "but I'm going to need some time."

"Take all the time you need, Sam. If you ration properly, you've got several days worth of food and water. But be advised, when your provisions run out, they won't be replenished."

"You'd let me starve?"

"Your health, like Rachel's, is in your hands. You are free to go as soon as you provide all eighteen access codes."

"You are aware," I say, "that the access codes only begin the process, correct? My clients are the only ones who can access the funds by entering a second code, known only to them."

"That being the case," the voice says, "it's not such a big deal for you to reveal them. And when you do so, we'll set you free."

"If I give you the codes, you'll kill me," I say.

"Not true."

"Prove it."

He pauses.

"We'll do that, Sam. All in good time."

I glance at Creed. He's still inspecting his enclosure, moving his hands across the surfaces, slowly but surely, inch by inch. I notice he hasn't pushed or hit or kicked the walls or thrown anything against them, as I did. Perhaps when he gets to that point, he'll realize there's no way out. Then maybe he'll give me some sort of signal or at least attempt to communicate.

I remove a sandwich from my cooler and begin eating. No need to worry about passing the metal tracking device Creed made me swallow. He's found me already, for whatever that's worth.

For the time being, I appear to be okay. While I'm not convinced they're going to let me go after I give them the codes, I'm encouraged that they're saying they will and even more encouraged by their comment about proving it to me "in good time."

Chapter 21

MANY HOURS HAVE passed. I have no way of knowing the exact number. I've been unable to sleep because the lights have been burning since the moment they were turned on. There is a ventilation system that recirculates the air every fifteen or twenty minutes. I still haven't powered up the computer in my cell. The voice has remained silent since making the promise about offering proof.

I glance at Creed's cell. In all this time, he's never taken his eyes or hands off the walls. He's lying on the floor now, moving his hands along the bottom edge. He's really pissing me off . I wonder how long he intends to touch the glass before trying to do something useful.

Suddenly, the lights go off and stay off for a couple of minutes. When they come back on, Creed's truck begins moving. I wonder why they don't want me to see the driver, but I'm thinking that's a good thing. If they intended to kill me, they wouldn't care if I could identify them, right?

His truck moves toward the far wall, maybe a hundred feet away, and the lights go off again. This time, they stay off for—I'm guessing now—fifteen minutes. When they come back on, Creed's cage is covered with a black tarpaulin. Then the garage-type door opens again and another truck enters.

They're going to show me Rachel!

The voice clicks on. "Sam, stand by. We're going to make a gesture of good faith."

The back part of the truck is covered with a red tarpaulin. It comes to a stop at an extreme angle, with a portion of the back facing me. Then another truck enters through the same door. This one has a blue tarp covering the truck bed. The driver of this truck positions it in such a way that our three trucks have formed a triangle, with my truck being the base. The lights go out again for a few minutes, and when they come on, I see that a small section of tarp on each truck has been cut away in such a manner I can see one person in each cage and they can see me.

But they can't see each other.

The two people are Rachel and Karen Vogel. Karen sees me and immediately starts sobbing and banging on her glass. Rachel appears to be cursing me.

The voice says, "This should be interesting, Sam. Keep in mind, they can't see each other or hear each other; nor can they hear you."

Suddenly, I can hear both women through my speakers. Karen is shouting, "Sam! Sam! Can you hear me?"

I look at her and nod. Then I look at Rachel. She's following my gaze but can't see anything because her blue tarp is blocking her vision. She has no idea there's a truck, a cage, or a woman less than ten feet away. As I turn back to Karen, I can see her also trying to follow my vision.

"What's there, Sam? Are you safe?" she says.

"Look at me, you son of a bitch," Rachel hisses. *"Look at me!"* she shouts.

I look at her.

She struggles to make her voice steady. "You can hear me?"

I nod.

"Give them the fucking codes and let's get out of here," she says.

I know Rachel can't hear me so I mouth the words, "Are you okay?"

"Why can't I hear you?" she says.

I glance at Karen. "Who are you talking to?" she says. "Can you hear me, Sam?"

I nod.

Rachel says, "Who the fuck are you talking to?"

I sigh. The voice was right. It *is* interesting.

Karen says, "Sam, look at me. Are *you* okay?"

I mouth, "I'm fine. Are you okay?"

"I can't hear you, Sam. I'm scared. What's happening?"

I shake my head while mouthing the words, "I don't know."

"Sam?" she says. "Can you still hear me?"

"Yes."

"I love you."

I bite my lip.

"Do you love me?"

I nod. "Yes."

Rachel says, "Sam, look at me. What's going on? Who are you talking to?"

I gesture toward my ears to imply I can no longer hear her.

My captor's voice says, "Chicken shit."

I say, "No kidding."

In my cell, Rachel's and Karen's voices suddenly go mute.

The voice says, "Sam, we've shown good faith. Now it's your turn."

"What do you mean?"

"We've proven to you that Rachel is alive and unharmed. And we've shown you Karen as a bonus."

"So what?" I say. "You said you'd give me proof that you'll let us go."

"That's not quite what I said. But let's not split hairs. We're still willing to let you go if you enter the codes."

"What about Rachel and Karen?"

"We have plans for all of you," the voice says. "But those plans depend entirely on your cooperation."

"What kind of plans?" I say.

"For now, we're going to play a little game," the voice says. "We'll start by having you turn on your computer."

I pause a minute. The voice says, "We're not kidding around, Sam. Just power up your computer and look at the screen. The rest is up to you."

I sit on the floor and put the computer in my lap. I glance at the two girls and see their mouths moving a hundred miles an hour. I can tell they're both asking me over and over if I can hear them. Jesus, you'd think they'd get a clue. *No, I can't fucking hear you!* I say in my head.

I power up the computer. Moments later, I hear the familiar tune that tells me it's ready. A screen appears with the numbers one through eighteen, one under the other. To the right of each number, there are sixteen white boxes and a larger yellow box. I'm supposed to put the codes in the boxes. I wonder what the yellow boxes are for.

Ah, I realize. *The names.*

I instantly start typing on the keypad, trying to find a way to get online. But I can't even get beyond this screen.

"Your computer is locked," the voice says.

"I'm not going to give you the codes," I say.

"You might want to reconsider."

"Why's that?"

"Because if you don't give us at least one of the codes in the next sixty seconds, we're going to remove the girls' covers, turn on their speakers, and tell each of them what you've been up to with the other."

"They're going to find out anyway," I say. "It's just a matter of time."

"Is that your final answer?" the voice asks.

I lean to my right and look at Creed's truck.

"He's not going anywhere," the voice says.

"Okay," I say.

"Good choice. Now enter a code."

"No," I say. "I meant okay, you can remove the tarps and tell the girls what I've been up to."

I think I hear the voice sigh. "It's your funeral," he says.

The lights go out.

Chapter 22

WHEN THE LIGHTS come on, the tarps have been removed. Now I can see both cages, both girls, and they can see each other. They stare at each other and then at me. The voice says, "They can see each other, but we haven't turned on their speakers yet. It's not too late, Sam. Karen doesn't know you're married, and Rachel doesn't know you're cheating. Type in a code, and we'll tell them a story to get you off the hook."

I look at the girls. Each of them saw me talking to someone else. Now they know it was the other girl.

"Fuck it," I say. "I'm toast."

"Very well," the voice says. "But rest assured, you *will* give us the codes. And soon."

"We'll see."

"We will indeed."

The girls' mikes and speakers are activated, as are mine. We can all hear each other. Rachel starts things off. "Who are you?" she says to Karen. To me, she says, "You *know* her? Who *is* she?"

Karen says, "Sam, I don't understand. Please tell me what's going on. I love you, Sam."

I sigh, thinking, *Oh shit!*

Rachel says, "You *what?* What the fuck did you just say?"

Karen says, "Sam, who *is* this woman?"

"She's—"

"I'm his *wife!*" Rachel says. "And you—what?—you *love* him? You're fucking my *husband?*"

Karen starts to say something to Rachel, changes her mind, and looks at me. She's frightened and confused. "Sam," she says. "Please. It's not true. It *can't* be true."

I grimace at Karen to show how pained I am to have to reveal it to her this way, in this setting. It's a sincere look. I'm honestly in pain over this. But of course, she is too, and her pain is ten times greater.

"You're *married?*" she says.

When I fail to answer, Karen bursts into tears. She covers her face with her hands and sobs. Her shoulders and upper body shake and heave. "No!" she cries. "Oh God, no!" Then she says, "Why? Oh my God, Sam. *Why?*"

"*Why?*" Rachel sneers. "He probably likes fucking you, that's why." She narrows her eyes and looks at me. "Don't you, Sam?"

I give my wife an angry look. "What's that?" Rachel says. "You *do* like fucking her? Or you *don't?* Which is it?"

Karen lowers her hands slightly and looks up at me. Apparently, this is something she would like to hear.

"Yes," I say.

"Yes?" Rachel says. "Yes, what?"

"I like fucking her."

"You're a lying, cheating bastard!" Rachel hisses.

"Sam," Karen says. "Please. I love you. Tell me that what we have is real."

I look at Rachel. She says, "I can't believe you've been fucking this piece-of-shit whore. *When* did you fuck her—while I'm at work every day? In some hotel room?" She gives Karen a withering look. "Or maybe you offer a discount for in-call at your place."

Karen says, "I don't even know what that means."

Rachel turns back to me and spits her words. "Real classy, Sam."

The three of us are quiet a moment, though Karen continues whimpering. Rachel finally breaks the silence. Her voice has changed. She's no longer screaming. She seems sad, hurt.

"These bastards kidnapped me," she says, "slapped me around, threatened me. And all the shit I was going through, terrified, I kept thinking about you. No matter what they did to me, I thought I was going through it for you." She lowers her eyes. "I never would have taken you for a cheat. With all your flaws, this is something I never saw coming. What a fool I am."

"Rachel, I—"

"Oh, shut up, you son of a bitch."

Karen says, "Sam—"

I say, "I'm sorry, Karen. I should have told you."

"*Her?*" Rachel says, suddenly angry again. "You should have told *her?* You should have told *me*, you son of a bitch!"

"You told me you loved me," Karen says.

Rachel gives me a hard-as-nails look.

"I *do* love you," I say.

Karen says, "You do?"

Rachel says, "*Excuse* me?"

"It's complicated," I say.

"You no-good fucking bastard," Rachel says.

At which point, the voice interrupts us, saying, "Sorry to break in, people, but it's time to take this to the next level."

Chapter 23

"WHO ARE YOU?" Rachel says to the voice. "Why are you holding *me*? I don't have the fucking codes!"

"What are they talking about, Sam?" asks Karen. "What codes?"

I look down at my feet, ashamed. "It's complicated," I say.

The voice says, "Ladies, allow me to explain. As you may know, Sam has developed a system to hide money from the authorities. By our estimate, he controls at least eight billion dollars for his clients, most of whom are terrorists, murderers, and thieves. The reason we're all here, my associates and I want that money. Sam has the access codes. All he has to do is type in the eighteen codes, and we'll set him free."

"What about *me*?" Rachel says. "I'm not involved in any of this. Why are you keeping *me* here?"

The voice says, "You're here to help motivate Sam to do the right thing."

I say, "What's the next level?"

The voice says, "You wanted proof we'd let you go. But we can't let you go until you give us the codes. So we're going to do the next best thing: we'll give you the opportunity to save one of your women."

All three of us are visibly shaken. I say, "What's that supposed to mean?"

"Choose one of them, Sam."

"Choose one for what?" I say.

"Choose one of them to live."

I look at Karen and Rachel. They're wearing matching expressions of horror. I'm sure I look just as bad. I start retching. The sandwich I ate is trying to come back up. I jump to my feet and force myself to gain control of my body.

"I'm not going to sentence one of them to die," I say.

There was a momentary pause. "You're certain about that?" the voice says.

The girls are making all sorts of sounds, I'm sure, but I can't hear them. My captors have turned off their microphones. The girls are both terrified, of course. I can see them banging their fists on the wall. I'm not an accomplished lip-reader, but the word "Sam" is pretty easy to decipher. They're both screaming my name. I'm standing in my cage, turning both palms down to show them a "try not to worry" gesture.

"I'm certain," I tell the voice. "I'm not going to sentence one to die."

Another pause, this one longer than the previous one, and then, with a weary, almost defeated tone, the voice says, "Very well, Sam. We'll kill them both."

I'm not sure of much that's happened since whenever it was I made love to Karen in the hotel room, which could have been today, yesterday, or a week ago. But I am sure of one thing: these guys, my captors, need me. They're not going to kill Karen and Rachel. At least not until they've gotten my codes.

"You're bluffing," I say.

The voice says, "Sam, we had to disconnect the microphones while we made an adjustment. In a moment, you'll hear a whirring sound coming from the ladies' cells. That sound is a vacuum pump, and it will be removing the oxygen from their cells. Once the pump powers up, the microphones will come back on, and you'll be able to hear their last words."

I shake my head. "That's absurd," I say. "Nice try, though."

I look at Rachel and Karen, wink, and make a circle with my thumb and forefinger to show them everything is okay.

Then the sound comes on, and I can hear the vacuum pumps sucking the air out of their containers.

Chapter 24

ADDRESSING THE VOICE, I say, "And now I'm supposed to believe that all the air is being sucked out of their
cubicles? Not possible."

The voice says, "Sam, you've got a scientific mind; you
should be able to follow this. Think of these cells as vacuum
storage containers like the ones you might use in your
kitchen, to keep things fresh. You, Rachel, Karen, Donovan
Creed—you've all been placed in hermetically sealed plastic
storage containers. Every twelve minutes since you became
our guest, we've pumped fresh air into your cell. The new
oxygen-rich air forces the carbon dioxide-laden air out. If we
stop pumping fresh air in, you'd survive maybe three or four
hours."

I look at the containers holding Rachel and Karen.
Both women are sitting on the floor. Their mouths are moving, but they appear lethargic. It doesn't seem possible they

could be affected to this degree in such a short period of time. I search my brain, trying to come up with an alternate theory. I think I might have one.

"If you suck all the air out of the containers, the walls will implode," I say, having no idea if this theory makes the slightest bit of sense.

"Sam, once again, we'd ask you to think about the vacuum storage containers used in kitchens all over the country. Those containers are also plastic. When you attach a pump to the rubber valve on top, you can vacuum seal the container. That's the whole idea behind keeping the food fresh for a longer period of time. In the same manner, each of our containers is equipped with a check valve in the floor that allows air to be pumped in one direction only. We've already turned on the pumps, and they will make short work of the air quality. We don't have to remove all the air, just enough for them to suffocate. Which they're about to do. But don't take my word for it. Here, I'll turn on the microphones, and you can hear for yourself. On the bright side, your women will be almost perfectly preserved. You'll hardly be able to tell they're dead."

The mikes go on, and I can hear them suffocating. It's excruciating. I ask myself if it's possible they're in on it, that they're faking. Rachel, the woman I loved more than any other, is lying on her side, her back to me. If she's faking, she's not even trying to let me see the effect the treatment is having on her. Karen is on her back, in a reclining posture, her torso propped up on her elbows. She's looking at me in horror, as if she's just met a demon in an alley. She's probably wondering what sort of monster would allow this to happen to her. She's no longer saying my name. She's gasping for breath. It appears to be a major effort for her to get even a half breath. She still looks beautiful, but she's aged five years in the last two minutes.

Karen's head hits the floor, and I can't bear it any longer.

"Okay, okay," I say. "I believe you. I'll enter the codes. Please stop."

The voice says, "Sam, you don't have time to enter all the codes. Enter one and I'll stop the process."

I enter the code of a man who is almost certainly a terrorist and hope they don't have a way to access his money. Nothing's worse than an angry terrorist.

"We need the name, Sam."

How did they know what I typed? They must have a keystroke link set up that bypasses the Internet. Is that possible? Or maybe they've written some code to block me from accessing the Internet.

"The name, Sam. Your ladies are near death."

I look at the cages. He's right. There's not much movement to see and no sounds left to hear.

I type in the name of the terrorist and instantly hear the vacuum pump stop.

There's a slight pause. Maybe they're checking the name against some sort of list. I don't give a shit about the codes anymore. I'm staring into the girls' cages, praying they're okay.

The voice finally says, "Thank you, Sam. That's a good start. We're pleased. In fact, we're so pleased we're going to give you another chance to save one of the women."

"What are you talking about? I gave you the code."

"We're past that, Sam. It's time to choose."

My heart hammers in my chest. If I hadn't been sitting, I would have certainly fallen to the floor.

"N ... No!" I stammer. "Look, I'll give you the codes ... and the names. I'll give you the codes and the names. I'll even help you rob them. I'll do whatever. But please. You have to let them go. It's not their fault. They've done nothing to you, nothing wrong. Please. I'm into it now. It's over. I'll do whatever you say. Let them go."

"Sam, your eloquence is touching, if tedious. Tell you what, we'll pump a little air into their containers each time you give us a code."

I enter the codes and names as quickly as possible and then turn my attention to the girls. They're still lying on the floors of their containers. I can't detect any movement or hear any sounds of breathing.

"Are they okay?"

"They're lucky," the voice says. "Another minute, they might have suffered brain damage."

A half minute passes before Karen starts moving. A few seconds later, Rachel screams. Over the next few minutes, both girls vomit. Now they're crying. Their actions and responses are practically mirror images of each other. Finally, I hear Karen speak.

"Sam ... are you okay?"

I want to shrivel up and slink away. This incredible goddess—the one I tricked into sleeping with me, the one I betrayed, the one who nearly died just now because of my greed—is actually worried about *me*. Rachel, on the other hand, has grown mute. She's sitting in the corner of her cell, arms hugging her knees. Her face is pale. She appears on the brink of throwing up again.

"Your women appear to be fully recovered," the voice says. "I'll give them a few minutes to compose their thoughts."

"W ... What are you talking about?" I say.

"Time to choose, Sam. We're going to give them a chance to plead for their lives. You get to play God today; you'll hear what they have to say, and then you'll decide which one gets to live."

Both women scream in protest, though each scream is unique. As they continue to beg our prison master to reconsider, I feel the bands around my chest tighten, as if I'm being constricted by a giant python. I look at my two women and can't believe this is happening. I can't believe it's come to this. My heart feels too large for my chest. I've reached my limit. I can't allow this to happen. There must be something I can do or say to stop the madness.

"Kill me instead," I say.

Both girls stop begging. There is complete silence as the voice seems to consider my request. Moments pass, moments that allow me to wonder if this is the end for me. As one of the most selfish people in the world, I've just shocked myself by offering to exchange my life for theirs. It's the right thing to do, but I haven't exactly made a life out of doing the right thing.

But I'm serious. I would rather die than have to sentence a loved one to death. The voice comes back in all three containers.

"Sorry, Sam. We like it better the other way. Girls, take a few minutes to compose your thoughts. We'll flip a coin to see who goes first. You'll each have one minute to convince Sam why he should choose you instead of the other one."

Chapter 25

THE PRISON MASTER turns off the girls' microphones. They take a moment to look at each other. While they do that, I try to imagine what must be going through their minds.

Until recently, Rachel thought she was married to a loyal, hardworking, successful man. True, the last six months or so, she'd grown distant, but things never got so bad that we felt the need to talk about it. In other words, we weren't ready for a marriage counselor. By and large, her life was stable, predictable, and reasonably content. But this last day or so has found Rachel going through a rough patch. In this short time frame, she's been kidnapped, slapped around, threatened, and forced to strip. She's learned her husband has been cheating on her and had to meet the "other" woman. She's been suffocated nearly to death, and now she's being forced to beg me to spare her life—me, the guy who caused all these terrible things to happen to her.

Thank God she hasn't yet learned that her only sister has been murdered.

Again, my fault.

Nor has the last day or so been a picnic for Karen Vogel. This singular beauty fell in love with a man she thought was loyal, wealthy, and single. She trusted me, slept with me, and found a dead man in her trunk. She's been kidnapped and threatened and discovered she's been dating a married man. She's been forced to meet my wife, has been nearly killed, and now finds herself in the position of having to beg me to spare her life—me, the guy who caused all these terrible things to happen to her.

Rachel turns away first. She goes to her cooler, takes out a bottle of water, and drinks it greedily. That must seem like a good idea to Karen, because she does the same. Rachel glares at me a few seconds before going back to the spot she seems to prefer, with her back touching the far wall. She still has on the suit she'd worn to work, a lightweight black Italian tweed with a shawl-collared jacket. The matching skirt would have stopped about two inches above the knee had she been standing. But she slides down the wall now and assumes her former posture of hugging her knees close to her chest. This is not a time for modesty, nor is it appropriate for me to notice, but she is inadvertently flashing her panties. Maybe I'm noticing because of the photograph I'd seen this morning—or yesterday, or whenever it was. They'd used a body double with black panties and the white bra with Karen's initials. In light of all that's transpired since that moment, I have to wonder why they went to so much trouble. What was the point of the photograph? I'll probably never know.

At any rate, Rachel is not wearing black panties today. They're tan, like the ankle-wrapped sandals she'd removed earlier to bang against the wall when trying to get my attention.

Karen is pacing the floor. She keeps glancing at me, giving me hopeful looks. She's scared, but there's hope in her eyes. She knows she has the advantage. She's younger, prettier, nicer, and has no baggage. I look at Rachel again. Her eyes are shut tight, and she's rocking a bit and appears to be moaning. I wonder if she's wishing she hadn't been so distant these last few months. I don't like the position I'm in, can't stand the thought of having to choose one of these women to die, but somewhere inside of me—God help me!—there's a tiny voice that wonders if Rachel might be rethinking the way she's treated me since being in the cubicle. It couldn't possibly escape her notice that while she was cursing and bitching and begging our captors to set her free, Karen was saying she loved me. Indeed, the first words out of Karen's mouth when regaining consciousness were to ask me if I was okay. I'm not proud to admit to that tiny voice inside me, but I'd be lying if I didn't tell you that some part of me is actually looking forward to hearing what Rachel might say to me. Will she beg for her life? Of course she will. Will she mean it? That's the billion-dollar question, isn't it?

I watch Karen gather the blanket around her. She's using it to shield herself as she pees. Rachel notices her too. She sneers and shakes her head in disgust, and I have a strong feeling these two could share a foxhole for the duration and never be friends.

The voice interrupts my thoughts.

"We tossed a coin. Rachel, you get to go first. Remember, you have one minute to make your case. Sam, pay attention."

Chapter 26

RACHEL STANDS AND crosses the floor in her bare feet. She places her hands on the Lucite wall. She's standing as close to me as she can, and she gives me a sort of half smile and says, "Sam, I don't know quite what to say. We've been together all these years, and I've always tried to be there for you. If someone had told me a week ago that you had the power to decide my fate, I wouldn't have worried for one second, because I thought you loved me as much as I've always loved you.

"Now, I'm not so sure. I look at the cell across from me and I see a woman who's younger than me, prettier than me, a woman who says she loves you. And worse, a little while ago, I heard you say that you loved her.

"I can't tell you how badly my heart hurts right now. Try to put yourself in my position. All I've done to be here is to love you. A part of me understands why you cheated. I know I haven't been the most attentive wife in the world, but you know I've always been faithful to you and I've never stopped loving you. And, Sam, I love you still.

"I'm not going to lie. If you choose to let me live, we're going to have some stressful times. I can't promise we'll make it. But I promise I'll try.

"Baby, I know at one time you loved me with all your heart. If there's still a spark inside you that wants me, I'd like the chance to live. I won't beg you, but I'd like to think my husband feels I'm worth saving. If you feel differently, I hope you know that I have always loved you and always will."

She removes her wedding ring, kisses it, puts it back on her finger, presses her lips together, and nods. When she nods, I see tears spill from her eyes. She moves back to her spot against the far wall but remains standing.

The voice says, "Karen, Rachel took twelve extra seconds. You can have the same."

Karen is wearing white thresher-cut jeans that have a pale blue tie-dye pattern running through them. She has on a matching blue tube top and blue strappy sandals with stiletto heels. Like Rachel, Karen moves to the closest point of her cubicle so she can look into my eyes. She says, "Sam, I hate them for putting you in this position. I'm not happy you didn't tell me about being married, but I love you. I love you, Sam, and I'm sure you didn't consider yourself married in your heart when you were with me. I never would have gone out with you if you'd told me, and that's probably why you decided not to. But we did go out, and I fell in love with you, and that hasn't changed.

"I don't want your wife to die, I swear to God I don't. But if it has to be one of us, wouldn't it be better to choose the one that represents your future instead of your past? She's had her chance. If she'd treated you the way you deserve, you never would have strayed in the first place.

"I don't want her to die, Sam. I do not want her to die. But I don't want to die either. You and I still have a chance to build a life together. I don't know if your wife wants children or not, but you told me that you do. And I do too, but not until you're ready. Because until you're ready for children, you've got every inch of this ..."

She quickly begins removing her clothes and doesn't stop until she is completely naked, save for the stiletto sandals. Then she says, "Sam, this is yours. It's yours whenever you want it. I swear to God I will make you the happiest man who ever lived. Please choose me. Please, Sam, I'm begging you, begging you to spare my life—so I can give it to you."

Karen stood at the glass, legs shoulder-length apart, arms out to either side, like da Vinci's Vitruvian Man, except that Karen looks a million times hotter than the guy in the drawing.

The voice says, "Sam, you've got a tough decision to make. But it's time."

I say, "You can't expect me to do this. It's inhuman."

"Sam, you shouldn't look at it like you're causing a death. Because what you're really doing is saving a life. Unfortunately, if you don't make a choice between your wife and mistress in the next ten seconds, we're going to kill them both. Shall I begin the countdown?"

I close my eyes, take a deep breath, and let it out completely, along with my soul.

"Not necessary," I say. "I've made my decision."

Chapter 27

I LOOKED AT Karen. Though she's been through a lot, I doubt she's ever looked so beautiful.

"Karen," I say, "I'm sorry. For everything."

Her face falls. She starts crying. Loudly at first, but then she nods her head, resigning herself to her fate. She cries softly another minute and then realizes she's still naked. She steps awkwardly into her panties, keeping her left hand on the wall to steady herself. She nearly trips trying to get her jeans on and then gives up, sits on the floor, and removes her sandals.

When she's finally dressed, the voice says, "Karen, you've been a good sport. If it's any consolation, we would have chosen you."

Karen shrugs and says, "You still can, you know."

The voice says, "Is there anything you wish to say to Sam before we start the vacuum pump?"

She looks at me and sighs. "I guess this proves you never would have left your wife for me. If you care, I think you made the wrong decision."

"I'm sorry, Karen," I say. "So, so sorry. I wish to God there was something I could do."

The voice says, "Sam, we've got to know. What made you choose Rachel?"

I look at my wife. For the first time since the decision was announced, she looks in my direction. I think she was so convinced I'd choose Karen, the idea that she's safe hasn't sunk in yet.

"We've had our share of problems," I say, "but we've got history. Maybe she hasn't been perfect, but I haven't either. I want a second chance, and I'm hoping she gives me one."

"Well, you'll soon have a chance to find out. Karen?"

"Yes, sir?"

"Sit tight awhile. We're going to take this in a different direction for a minute."

All three of us look at each other, wondering what fresh hell the voice has in store for us.

The voice says, "Sam, you've already made your choice, so there's no turning back. However, it might interest you to know that Rachel has a secret of her own."

Rachel's face drains itself of all color.

The voice continues, "Rachel, would you like to tell Sam what you've been up to? Or shall we?"

Somewhere in my brain, a puzzle piece is trying to fall into place. I can't quite make it fit, but as I watch Rachel standing in her cell, pale-faced and visibly squirming, I know the missing piece is a person:

Donovan Creed.

He's the one who said he'd save me. I asked if he would save Rachel and he said, "Sam, when it all goes down, if that's what you want, I'll save Rachel too."

Later he'd said, "I'll help you get her back, *if that's what you want*," which means Creed knew about Rachel. Whatever I'm going to hear about her, Creed already knows. He promised to save me and said he'd save Rachel too—*if that's what I wanted*.

Despite the death-level of stress I've been subjected to—add to that what I'm about to learn about Rachel—I suddenly see the slightest glimmer of hope. Creed's promise to get me out of here, with Rachel, if that's what I want, suddenly feels possible. I glance across the parking lot at the black, tarp-covered cage that holds Creed and wonder if he's still alive. If so, I wonder if he's still moving his hands over the Lucite surfaces, searching for a weakness in the structure.

Then, just as quickly, I lose all hope, because I just caught that other little thought that was running around in my brain—the one where I'm about to pull into my driveway and Creed tells me to hurry up because there's not much time to get to the secret room. During which time, Creed once again tells me he'll save me, but he says, "If what?"

And I had answered, "If I don't let them steal your money."

And, of course, I had let them steal his money. I'd given them the codes, all of them, including Creed's. But wait—

wasn't there a sub-clause, a caveat that might yet make my life worth saving?

Yes! Donovan Creed had told me to make sure I gave them his code last.

Had I?

The voice says, "Very well, Rachel, I'll do it for you. I'll tell Sam and Karen what you've been up to. But first, we'll need a moment to set the stage."

Again, the sound and lights go out.

When they come back on, the garage door opens and another truck comes in, with another tarp-covered cage. Karen's and Rachel's cages are moved to make room for this new cage. The lights go out so the drivers can exit without being seen, but the green tarp on the new cage remains in place. I guess our captors' flair for drama continues.

The voice says, "Hmm ... so many ways to tell the story, where shall I begin?"

Karen is a creature of curiosity. Though her execution has been stayed momentarily, she approaches the area of her cubicle that affords the best view of Rachel's face. She, too, seems interested in what's behind the green tarp. Rachel isn't looking at the new cage. She seems to know what's inside.

The voice says, "Sam, your wife wasn't entirely honest with you earlier when begging for her life."

Rachel pretends to be unconcerned. She retrieves a sandwich from the cooler and starts opening it. She waves her hand in the general direction of the new cage and says, "Fuck it. Doesn't matter now. Tell them whatever you want."

Chapter 28

THE VOICE SAYS, "Sam, you may have noticed Rachel has been a bit distant the past six months. I can shed some light on that: she's been having an affair of her own."

I study my wife's face. Could it be true?

She looks at me while taking a bite of her sandwich. A small, wry smile starts tugging at the corner of her mouth, a smile that says two can play this game.

How could she have sounded so sincere moments ago when pleading for her life?

"I probably haven't been the most attentive wife in the world, but you know I've always been faithful to you ..."

When had she learned to lie so convincingly?

Karen Vogel flashes me a look of sadness that says, *Can you believe this?* She says, "I'm sorry, Sam."

The voice interrupts its story about Rachel long enough to say, "Karen, you are truly one of a kind."

Rachel says, "Oh, go fuck yourself."

The voice continues, "Speaking of fucking ..."

He proceeds to tell us that a businessman named Kevin Vaughn is in the cage under the green tarp. Kevin hired Rachel's company to produce a marketing campaign for a new product. Rachel was on the ad committee. They met, fell in love, blah, blah, blah. The voice doesn't say, "Blah, blah, blah," but it may as well have. My gut is churning. I am dying inside. I'd just chosen Rachel, and by doing so, I'd sentenced Karen to die.

And Karen feels bad for me!

Rachel says, "This is such bullshit. There's no way Kevin is in that cage. That's why you're keeping it covered."

The voice says, "Sam, be advised that Rachel and Kevin's affair is not what you'd term casual. We've purposely made it impossible to tell time while in the cell, but I can tell you now that it's nighttime, and your whole drama began two nights ago. You thought it began yesterday morning when you met Karen at the hotel. But think about how Rachel was acting the night before. How would you describe her state of mind, Sam?"

I don't want to have this or any other conversation with my captor. But I can't help myself. I remember having these same thoughts yesterday when I spoke to her on the phone. *She'd been pacing the floor from the time I'd gotten home to the time she went to bed. When I walked in the kitchen last night, she'd been on her cell phone, agitated. I saw her try to make a call over and over, though she never left a message. At one point, she'd been in her closet with the door closed. When I entered, I saw her sitting on the floor, eyes filled with tears, cell phone in her lap. I'd asked what was going on. She'd told me to leave her alone.*

"Sam?" The voice is relentless.

"She was highly agitated," I say.

"Would you like to know why?"

"How about you humor me until I beg you to stop?"

The voice says, "That's the night she paid the hit man to kill her sister, Mary."

Chapter 29

RACHEL, STUNNED, LETS her sandwich fall to the floor. Whatever she'd thought the voice was going to reveal about her, this wasn't part of it. Rachel's face is contorted with pain. She rolls on the floor and starts sobbing. She's on her side, kicking the wall of her cubicle, convulsing and repeating her sister's name over and over.

I need to speak, need to ask something, but I can't seem to cough out the word. I try twice to get it out of my throat. Finally, it comes, as if everything will make sense if I can utter this one simple word: "Why?"

The voice answers, "Mary found out about Rachel and Kevin. She was going to tell you. Rachel didn't want you to find out, so she hired a hit man to kill Mary."

Rachel is writhing on the floor in anguish. Karen looks at me, pity in her eyes.

The voice says, "You remember seeing Mary at the park yesterday?"

I nod.

"She was waiting there for you, felt safer meeting in a public place. She brought a co-worker with her, dressed as a policeman."

The word comes easier this time. "Why?"

"Mary was afraid Kevin might follow you to the park and try something. She thought if Kevin saw her with a policeman, she'd be safe."

"But ... how did she know I was coming?" I say. "Wait a minute—" I look at Karen. "The guy dressed like a policeman. He was *your* friend."

Karen smiles broadly and takes a theatrical bow. To the voice, she says, "Does this mean I'm done here?"

The voice says, "I suppose it does. Hang on a sec, we'll drive you out. Sorry about the vacuum pump. We had to make it seem real."

Karen says, "No problem. I've been through worse."

Rachel and I are staring at each other, our mouths hanging open.

"What the fuck is going on?" I say, **finally.**

"Your worst nightmare," the voice answers.

The room goes dark a moment and then light. Then Karen's truck starts driving her away. As we watch her rolling toward the door, we hear her say, "Take care, Sam. You too, Rachel." Then she says, "It's been a wild ride, hasn't it?"

When the garage door closes behind her, I say, "This whole thing was a setup. And Karen was in on it from the word go."

The voice says, "Ya think?"

Rachel says, "This is bullshit! You've got your codes. Stop playing with us. Take your money and leave us alone!"

The voice says, "We've got one more game for you."

Rachel says, "Fine. Just do it. Whatever it is, get on with it."

The voice says, "Rachel, I think you're going to enjoy this game. Sam? Not so much."

Chapter 30

"RACHEL," THE VOICE says, "Kevin has just regained consciousness.

Would you like to see him?"

Rachel perks up. "You mean he's really in there?"

"He is."

"Then yes!" she says. "Please!"

She glances at me, shows me a half frown, and shrugs.

They do that thing with the lights going off a minute and then back on. From my vantage point, I can't see Kevin the businessman and wife fucker. But Rachel can, and she likes what she sees. Tears of joy are streaming down her cheeks. "Oh God," she says, "Oh God! Oh God! I thought I'd lost you!"

I've heard a lot of ominous statements these last thirty hours, but none that hit me as hard.

The voice says, "Rachel, Sam chose to save your life, so you're good to go. The only question is which of these men will be going with you?"

"Excuse me?" I say.

"You had your chance to choose," the voice says, "now it's Rachel's turn."

Rachel and I exchange a look. I put everything I can into it, trying to get two years of courtship and six years of marriage into one look.

I say, "Rachel, you know I love you. I just proved it to you by picking you. You've cheated? Okay, fine, so have I. Let's start fresh. Let's end this shit and go home."

Rachel nods back at me and addresses the voice, "I don't have to go through all the motions like we did last time. For me, it's a simple decision. I choose Kevin. Do whatever you want to Sam."

I literally fall to the floor. I hold my head with both hands, squeezing hard to keep my brains from exploding.

"You're certain?" the voice says.

"Positive," Rachel says. "Sorry, Sam. We had some good moments. I'll try to remember them."

I scramble to my feet, make my way to the wall closest to her, and place my hand on the Lucite. "Rachel!" I shout. I make a show of removing my wedding ring, just as she'd done moments earlier. I kiss it and put it back on. "We're married," I say. "We're soul mates!"

It seems I've gotten through to her. Rachel looks long and hard at her wedding ring. She slowly spins it around her finger a couple of times, and I try to imagine what thoughts are playing in her head. I get my answer when she removes her wedding ring, kisses it, walks to her camping toilet, opens the lid, and tosses it in.

"I belong to Kevin now," she says. "Everything I am, everything I have, is his."

And that's when it hits me: all this time, the one piece of the puzzle I have never been able to understand has just fallen into place. The white bra with the "K" and "V" that had me so freaked out, it doesn't stand for Karen Vogel.

It stands for Kevin Vaughn.

The voice says, "Sam, would you like to have a chance to meet Kevin?"

"Fuck you!" I say. "Fuck you all."

Our captor must have the green tarp rigged to an electronic device because it falls away on its own. Kevin Vaughn and I stare at each other. He's about to say something, but Rachel interrupts him, saying, "Don't feel like you have to speak to him, Kevin. Just take me home now, honey, okay?"

I look in disbelief at the guy in the black Armani suit with the feathered, white-silk pinstripe. He's wearing a crisp white shirt and a fiery red tie with a matching pocket square. I look at his sissy haircut and sissy shoes and say, "Is that how it's going to be, Kevin? You've been sneaking around fucking my wife for six months, and now you're going to what—move into my house, set up housekeeping with a woman who killed her own sister? A woman who, without a second thought, sentenced her own husband to die?"

Kevin clears his throat and says, "I think when you say it that way, you're putting the worst possible face on the situation."

"Is that how they teach you to talk in advertising school?"

Rachel says, "He's not in the advertising business, you buffoon. I am. For your information, he owns a fifty-million-dollar company. How he talks is none of your business."

"What type of product were you working on with him, some new type of condom?"

"Don't be a sore loser, Sam."

"I saw a photograph of you on our kitchen floor. You were lying there in your bra and panties with a bondage ball in your mouth."

She thinks about it a moment. Then she smiles. "So?"

"What was that, some sort of sex game?"

"What's the matter, Sam, you jealous?"

"Maybe," I say. "But I couldn't help notice the picture was taken right around the time your sister was murdered."

"You're insane. Stop, Sam. You're embarrassing yourself."

I look at Kevin. "You took that picture?"

Kevin tilts his head slightly and shrugs.

"Asshole."

The voice says, "Sam, thank you for the input. Kevin, looks like you win the prize: freedom and the lovely Rachel. I know it was an inconvenience, putting you in the cage, but at least you learned that Rachel's love for you is sincere."

Can you believe this guy?

The voice continues, "Sam, we're sorry it wasn't much of a contest. We can't begin to understand how you must feel. But it's all water under the bridge at this point, yes?"

"Not quite," I say. "I've got a question for you, you vomitous piece of shit."

The voice says, "We don't believe 'vomitous' is a word. However, we're beginning to see Rachel's point about you being a sore loser."

"I don't care what you think about me," I say. "But how do you expect to activate the codes? You've only got the first half of the sequence."

The voice says, "Not true. We've always had the second sequence. They're embedded in your computer."

"That's not possible," I say.

"Think about it," the voice says. "During the past two years, every one of your clients has accessed some of their money at least once. You're an honest man, Sam. You set up your program in such a way that you couldn't see your clients' codes. But we're not so honest. We hacked into your system and found them—I won't try to explain how. But we had a problem: the accounts were all numbered. We were kidding about the codes. We never needed them; we had them all along. What we needed were the legal names on the accounts. Without those, we couldn't access the funds."

My head is swimming, but my captor's voice sounds confident.

"So that's it," I say.

"It is."

"What happens now?"

"We'll kill you quickly. With all the twists and turns that have been going on, Rachel and Kevin are going to want to make sure you're dead. After that, we'll reunite the happy couple and bring down the curtain on this play."

"Karen's getting a big cut?" I ask, wondering why that thought popped into my head.

Rachel muttered, "I knew she was a whore. But I suppose she earned it, having to fuck you."

"Are you in on it too, Rachel?" I say. "Are you getting a cut?"

The voice says, "Rachel is not a party to this drama. She only gets to live, along with whatever she inherits from your estate."

"You sound awfully smug," I say. "If you can't access the money at the last minute, you're going to wish you'd kept me alive."

"Sam," the voice says, "from the moment you gave us the names, my associates have been working furiously. It's over; we've already got the money."

"Maybe not all of it," I say. "What's the final take?"

The voice pauses, as if checking. After a moment, it says, "Nine billion four hundred million and change. That sound about right?"

Shit.

"Good for you," I say. "And fuck you all. Go ahead, throw the switch. I'll see you in hell."

"Until then, Sam," the voice says. There's a slight pause as my captors make the electronic adjustments to start the vacuum pump.

When it's ready, the voice says, "Sorry for the delay. We're good to go. Make your peace, Sam, I'll give you ten seconds."

"You get nine billion dollars, and I get ten seconds, huh?"

"Doesn't hardly seem fair, does it?"

"When does the countdown begin?"

"Now ... unless anyone has a final comment ... No? In that case—"

Kevin Vaughn clears his throat. "Actually, if I may, I'd like to ask Sam a quick question."

I look up at him and see Rachel doing the same. She looks as worried as I feel. She says in a pleading voice, "Kevin, we're so close. Please, hon, let's just end this and go home."

"What's your question?" I say.

<u>Part Two</u>

DONOVAN CREED

Chapter 31

TWO DAYS EARLIER, 9:30 am ...

I look at my watch and think about Sam Case who, at this very moment, is in a hotel room having sex with Karen Vogel. This, the best morning of his life, is about to turn into his worst nightmare. I'm in the Rock Creek Diner, by Seneca Park.

The bold writing atop the menu tells me all I need to know about the impending dining experience:

"Since 1947, we've served food as good, pure, wholesome, and consistent as a mother's love."

Jimmy Squint sits across the table, looking at me like my boss must be the craziest son of a bitch on Earth.

"Creed, your boss must be the craziest son of a bitch on Earth," he says, studying my face, waiting to hear the punch line.

There is none.

"So that's the plan," Jimmy says. "What am I missing?"

"I could tell it again," I say, "but it never gets any saner."

Our waitress, a beautiful little Southern girl named Macie, sets a platter of country ham biscuits between us and lingers long enough to show me the kind of smile she'll use someday to keep her man home at night. Of course, Jimmy Squint ruins the moment by saying, "Biscuits look a bit hard."

Jimmy might be right about my boss being crazy, but he is dead wrong about the biscuits. Nor does his remark sit well with the customers who overheard it. For his part, Jimmy doesn't seem aware of the grumbling and general unease building up around us.

"You're serious?" he says, back on the subject of the plan.

I nod.

"Guy's got that much money?"

"He does."

"But it ain't enough."

"It ain't," I say.

Jimmy Squint gives me his trademark squinty look, wondering if I might be mocking him. Unable to tell for certain, he moves the conversation along.

"Seems like a hell of a lot of trouble to go through."

I shrug.

Jimmy says, "This guy's got information you want, why not beat it outta him?"

I don't say anything.

Jimmy says, "Or round up his loved ones, kill 'em one at a time. Make him watch ... I don't care *who* he is, he'll talk."

"You'd think so," I say, just to have something to say.

"But your guy wants to walk the whole neighborhood just to kick the dog."

Jimmy Squint has an odd way of putting things, but I know what he means.

"No matter how you phrase it," I say, "it still comes out the same."

Our booth in the Rock Creek Diner has a large window that overlooks Seneca Park. From where we sit, we can see about eighty men and women and maybe a dozen kids, but curiously, no dogs.

Jimmy Squint takes a bite of a country ham biscuit. "Where's this whole shooting thing going down?" he whispers.

I nod at the window, indicating the park but get distracted by Jimmy's frown.

"It's not that the biscuits are hard," I say. "You're eating them the wrong way."

He gives me a look of bewilderment. "How many friggin' ways can a biscuit be eaten?"

"There's a protocol unique to this particular dining experience that should be observed," I say.

"A protocol," he says. "The fuck's that supposed to mean?"

"Your biscuit wants to be dipped in the gravy," I say.

He scrunches his face. "That's like, pure fat."

"You're in Kentucky, James. That's authentic redeye. Not fat."

He appraises the tiny porcelain vessel on his plate and frowns. "Why's it so dark?"

"It's made with coffee."

"*Coffee?*" he says, getting all worked up about it. "Who the hell puts coffee in their gravy?"

I hear a couple of chairs scrape the floor as a large man in coveralls and his unshaven wife jump to their feet a few tables behind Jimmy and set their bodies in some manner of backwoods fighting stance. The other diners who heard Jimmy's latest outburst are glaring at him, red-faced.

"The fuck you starin' at?" Jimmy Squint says to basically the entire diner.

At first, Jimmy's hands are at his sides, under the table. There is no discernable movement, but suddenly both his hands are on top of the table, the fingers of his right hand resting an inch away from a serrated steak knife. This happens instantly: no hands on the table and then two hands on the table, no time passing between the two events.

The standing man and woman spit into their palms and start rubbing their hands together. The man is about six-four and two-eighty, strong in that farmhand sort of way. The wife is shorter, but tougher, I think, and she has the shoulders.

"If it comes down to it, I'll take the farmer," I say.

"I think they're both farmers," Jimmy says.

He had me there. "You take the woman," I say.

"I still ain't sure which one you mean."

"One on the right."

The couple advances slowly toward our table while rolling up the sleeves of their long underwear. Jimmy hears something and spins his head toward me. "The fuck?"

Jimmy's hands aren't the only fast ones at our table. While he'd been sizing up the farmer's wife, I'd pulled a gun from beneath the table, ratcheted a live round into the chamber, and aimed it two feet from Jimmy Squint's face.

"Try the gravy," I say, and everyone goes quiet.

"What? This is bullshit!" Jimmy says.

"Reason they call it redeye," I say helpfully, "when you pour black coffee into the drippings, the evaporating gravy forms a red eye in the center of the frying pan."

Jimmy is a small, ferret-faced man with ferret-quick hands, probably the fastest hands I ever saw with a knife. But I'm not slow either, and we both know he can't grab the steak knife and reach across the table and stab me before I can squeeze off a shot. Not only that, but he was counting on me for a big payday with minimal work.

He curses incoherently, glances around the room, shrugs, grips a fresh biscuit from his plate, dips it in the red-eye gravy, and pops it into his mouth. Every eye in the diner watches him chew, waiting to see the transformation take place, as often happens when Yankees get caught up in the divine exhalation of Southern cooking. Sure enough, despite his annoyance over the forced feeding, a smile starts tugging at the corners of Jimmy Squint's mouth, and his eyes light up like a preacher spotting cash in the collection plate.

"That's damn good!" he says.

Farmer man cocks his head, waiting in case a smart-ass remark has been left unspoken.

"I must apologize for my guest," I say. "He's from Detroit." Farmer man and his wife look at each other and nod, as if that explained everything.

"That a real gun?" she says.

"It is," I say.

"Kinda puny," Farmer man says.

"Glock 26," I say. "Compact model, nine millimeter." They nod again, go back to their table, and work their large bodies back into their small chairs. A table of elderly women gives Jimmy the hard stare before tucking back into their biscuits. A young girl sitting alone at the counter shakes her head in sympathy and begins Twittering the adventure to her friends. Macie, our cute little waitress, seems relieved. I put the gun back into my ankle holster.

"So what you're saying," Jimmy Squint says, "you're being paid to basically fuck with this guy's life, and you're paying me twenty grand to, what—watch him? Follow him? Guard him?"

"All the above," I say.

"When's all this supposed to start?"

I look at my watch. "About ten thirty, give or take."

Jimmy motions for our waitress. "Honey," he says to Macie, "would you be a sweetheart and bring us another plate of biscuits?"

Several sets of eyes look up from their plates.

"And bring me a double order of that redeye gravy," he adds.

Chapter 32

"THIS GUY," Jimmy Squint says.

"Sam Case?"

Jimmy nods. "What's he drive?"

"Audi R8."

Jimmy nods approvingly. "Sweet ride," he says.

"It is that."

"Where's the rifle?"

"It'll be in the front seat waiting for you. Shoot twice and jump in the car. Lou will drive you to the hotel. When you get there, he'll show you your ride. Climb in, sit tight. Got it?"

Jimmy Squint nods. "I sure would like to drive that Audi one time."

Jimmy used to be a getaway driver for Frank Carbonne's crew back in Detroit. To this day, he harbors a fondness for fast cars. Along with his hands, Jimmy has fast feet that he used to tap out rhythms with the gas and brake pedals while being chased by cops or disgruntled mobsters.

"Maybe next time," I say.

The word on Jimmy was he didn't enjoy driving getaway unless someone was chasing him. More than once he'd angered his crew by taking unnecessary risks in order to provoke all-out chases. These acts included—but were not limited to—honking his horn, clipping the corner of a cop's car, and even taking the occasional shot at one.

At 10:00 am sharp, fifteen men walk into the diner wearing police uniforms. One steps forward to do the talking.

"Attention, everybody," he says. "My name's Officer Glen Denning, and this ..." He gestured toward me. "... is Donovan Creed, special agent for Homeland Security. We've got a situation about to go down in Seneca Park, and I'm going to ask for your cooperation, which means I'll need you to finish up your meals and be out of here in the next ten minutes."

The owner of the diner pops his head through the order window and says, "Make sure they pay their bills, Glen!"

Macie adds, "And tip me generous, in case they blow up the diner!"

Everyone laughs.

Officer Denning continues, "I'd appreciate it if you stay at least a mile away from the park for the next four hours. My men will keep the area contained, but it'll go a whole lot easier for us if you don't tell all your friends and relatives. Last thing we need is a bunch of gawkers getting in our way."

The patrons hadn't panicked when I pulled my Glock on Jimmy Squint awhile ago, so I don't figure they'll panic over this announcement. I'm right. They busy themselves with paying their bills and leaving. "Give 'em hell, Glen!" says one guy, and some of the others chime in with similar words of encouragement.

Officer Glen Denning nods somberly and says, "We'll do our jobs." He pauses before adding, "You can count on that."

After escorting the last of the diners to their cars, the cops change into civilian clothes and take up their positions along the perimeter of the park. A traffic control crew begins closing off the access streets, ensuring that Cannons Lane will be the only way in and out.

Before leaving to join his team, Officer Denning looks at me and says, "How'd I do?"

"That part at the end about doing your jobs," I say. "How long you practice that?"

"I know it wasn't part of the script," he says, "but I felt it added something, don't you?"

Jimmy Squint says, "What it's worth, I think they all bought it."

"Next time," I say, "if there is a next time ..."

The man playing the part of Officer Denning says, "Yes, sir?"

"Stick to the script."

Chapter 33

MOMENTS LATER, SALVATORE, Bonadello's driver, Shane, calls me from the limo. "Lou's got Sam's keys," he says. "The Audi should be there any minute."

"Where are you guys?" I ask.

"We're rolling," Shane says. "We're two miles from the Cannons exit. We'll be there in about ..." I imagined him checking his watch. "... four minutes."

Sal Bonadello is crime boss for the Midwestern United States. Since this whole thing started with a phone call from Rachel to Sal, he gets a big taste (a high percentage of the take), but I'm making him work for his piece. He's got a goon with him, a pasty muscleman with the street name Bald Eagle. Eagle's real name is Herbert, but who's going to take him seriously? Sal didn't want to use either of his regular bodyguards because they're too savvy. They might put together the size of the take and demand a lot more than Sal wants to pay. So while we wouldn't trust Eagle in a major role (he can't shoot for shit), he's big and strong and should be able to handle a bit part like the one we've outlined for him.

Sam Case is a local computer whiz who came up with the most ingenious method of moving money I've ever seen. He takes your nest egg and makes it not just untraceable, but invisible. Over a killing career spanning twenty years, I'd managed to accumulate approximately three hundred million dollars, most of it stolen from my victims—a sum of money that had become increasingly hard to hide from my government bosses. In my line of work, your bosses don't give you a gold watch when you retire. They give you a bullet and seize your assets.

Everyone who's ever done this sort of work plans for his or her retirement. We all put money away. Problem is, when you try to get your money, you get your bullet. When you call it quits with Uncle Sugar, the only way to stay alive is to stay away from your money. If you're resourceful, you can get away clean. But you can't get away with your money. Sooner or later, your money will lead them directly to you.

Enter Sam Case. When I heard about Sam's computer program, I knew I'd be able to protect my nest egg upon retiring. Protecting my life will still be up to me, but that's something I can handle.

I do contract killing for two people: the aforementioned Sal Bonadello and an angry, quadriplegic midget bent on global conquest named Victor. Victor is diabolical, incredibly brilliant, and quite possibly a billionaire.

Victor is also a client of Sam's. When I first heard of Sam's idea, I contacted Victor and had his people check it out. We both ended up placing a quarter billion with Sam, and that got us thinking about Sam's sixteen other clients. More than once, we speculated about stealing their assets, but we never put a plan to it.

Until fate stepped in.

More about that later ...

With less than four minutes till showtime, I send Jimmy Squint to his post, and I remain in my seat by the diner window to watch the scene unfold.

The limo appears right on schedule. The door opens, and Sam goes tearing across the grass. Mary and her co-worker, Chuck, the guy dressed up like a policeman, are on Reece, right where they're supposed to be, which tells me that Callie Carpenter has done her job perfectly. Callie, a gorgeous killing machine and longtime associate of mine, is currently playing the role of Sam Case's girlfriend. Callie had also befriended Chuck (just friends), and it was Callie who made sure Mary found out about Rachel's affair with Kevin Vaughn. Callie was the go-between for the meeting at Seneca Park.

Jimmy Squint shoots twice. One shot hits Mary's heart dead center; the other finds a home in Chuck's head. I'm not as casual about these killings as I might sound. In fact, I'm completely against them, which is why I refused the contract and passed it off to Jimmy instead. From the gutter grate on Reece Street, one of my marksmen shoots Chuck in the head with a paintball, in case someone happens to be watching from the wrong angle and thinks they've witnessed an actual shooting. Jimmy jumps into Sam's car and my assistant, Lou Kelly, drives the Audi back to the hotel and places the keys and the famous Rachel photograph in an envelope under the driver's seat. The photo is real, but it's been doctored. She's not actually tied to the floor, nor was the photo taken this morning at 8:46 am as the time and date stamp shows. The photo was taken by Kevin Vaughn several months ago. I found it, along with the bra, in the black plastic bag in Rachel's closet where she keeps the rest of her nasty outfits and sex toys. Want to know where she hides the plastic bag? In the giant hatbox on the top shelf of her closet—not the sort of place Sam would ever think to look.

Meanwhile, the crowd of actors in the park converges on Sam, but not too quickly, making sure he gets away. The two runners pretend to cut off his escape. Now Herbert—Bald Eagle—gets out of the car and fires two blanks in the general direction of the runners. They fall on cue, and Sam jumps over them as if he'd rehearsed the part. Sal Bonadello fucks with Sam about Rachel's bra size for awhile—which causes the extras in the park to have to adjust their chase—and finally lets him back in the car. They drive away leaving all this in their wake: two dead bodies, two guys pretending to be dead ... and eighty extras who witnessed a double homicide but are convinced the whole thing is a movie shoot.

Meanwhile, the director tells the extras to hold their positions while the film crew sets up on the far corner. The "cops" converge on the bodies from one side of Reece, the ambulance from the other, and the EMS guys load the bodies in the vehicle and drive away while the cameras roll. A cleaning crew hops out of a van and starts power washing the blood and paint off the street. When that's done, as the movie extras mill about, waiting for the scene to be shot with a new batch of actors, the paintball guy climbs out of the gutter and tells the rubes how he makes the "killing" look so realistic.

As I think about all this from your perspective, I can see I've gotten ahead of myself. I should probably back up and fill in some of the gaps for you, starting with Rachel and Kevin and how this whole idea came into being.

You've heard quite a bit about Rachel, and maybe you've formed an opinion of her, and that's fine; it's your decision to make. But like every story, there are two sides ...

Chapter 34

TWO YEARS AGO, when Sam Case explained his money-moving scheme to me, I decided to stay close and make certain he wasn't planning to scam me.

So I moved into his attic.

I've traveled all over the country the past two years, doing jobs for Homeland Security and various contract killings, but for the most part, I've been based in Sam and Rachel's attic. During that time, I spent many hours getting to know the Cases from behind the scenes. I learned their schedules, their routines—in fact, I learned more about them than they could possibly know about each other.

When Sam and Rachel were at work, I'd climb out of the attic and make myself at home. I'm not a snoop by nature, but rather a tireless investigator. In the early days, I started with the computers, spending weeks opening up files and sending them to my headquarters in Virginia so Lou

Kelly's geek squad could decipher them. When I'd gotten what I could electronically, I went through all the medicine cabinets and e-mailed the prescriptions to Lou so he could make the proper adjustments on Sam's and Rachel's medical records. I looked at every piece of paper in their house, from appliance manuals to address books to business and personal files to checkbooks. Why would I care about appliance manuals?

I don't.

But sometimes people will hide a phone number somewhere, like inside a book cover or within the pages of an appliance manual, and that phone number might lead to something important. So I opened every page of every book, searched every cabinet inch by inch, making certain there were no hidden cubbies. I scanned every photograph in the house, sent them to Lou to be indexed, and checked the frames they'd been in. I checked behind every print and painting on the walls. Over time, I sprayed every square inch of carpeting with a mixture of Luminol powder and hydrogen peroxide to check for blood. I pressed every inch of carpet checking for bulges. I moved furniture around to check those areas as well. I checked every square inch of molding and checked the baseboards and the air vents and returns. I took the filters out of the air conditioners to see if anything had been hidden behind them. I checked every square inch of every article of clothing, especially the pockets. I checked every piece of luggage, and all of Rachel's purses. In other words, I performed an exhaustive search, one that took me six months to complete. By comparison, you put a team of cops in a house this big and give them a search warrant, and they're done in six hours, tops. But they're going to miss a lot.

In the early days at Sam and Rachel's home, when I grew tired of reading, I drilled small openings and filled them with wireless pinhole cameras. There are more than sixty of them installed throughout the house. It takes me three hours every two weeks just to change the battery packs on those cameras! I also made minor repairs so they wouldn't have to call in repairmen. I took the time to make my attic area as comfortable as possible. I installed access doors in several areas of the house, siphoned some heat and air from the rooms they didn't use very often, and wired the attic for computer access. I linked to their land phones and their computers and even programmed a scanner to listen in on their cell phone calls.

Of course, it wasn't all work. Sam and Rachel are gone all day, five days a week, so I took the time to really enjoy their gorgeous home. Mondays and Fridays, they had a half-day cleaning service I had to watch out for. The other three mornings, I'd work out in their state-of-the-art gym for a couple of hours and then relax in the steam shower in their master bedroom. Afternoons were reserved for my investigating.

Usually, when I become an unseen part of my hosts' lives, I grow to hate them. Familiarity really does breed contempt. In this case, the more I learned about her, the more I found myself becoming intrigued with Rachel. This phenomenon started the day I learned she volunteered her time on Sunday afternoons at a horse farm that takes care of broken-down racehorses. I visited the place one day—not a Sunday—and took the full tour. I was so impressed by the work they did, I let a couple of months go by and then made a substantial anonymous contribution.

While monitoring Sam's and Rachel's lives by camera, computer, and phone, I saw how hard she tried to make their marriage work. Sam's a decent enough guy, but not the most romantic person in the world. He's a workaholic; he's forgetful and often insensitive. He's bad about following through on prior commitments he's made, such as meeting his wife after work or attending receptions for her clients. He's always up for his work but holds the opinion that her work is meaningless, since it contributes in such a small way to their income.

Rachel was showing all the classic signals of a bored, ignored wife, but Sam wasn't picking up on them. She felt unneeded and taken for granted. He craved sexual attention, she craved relationship attention, and neither got what they wanted.

Over time, I saw them slip further and further away from each other. By the time they were sleeping in separate bedrooms, I knew things were beyond repair. She'd climb into her bed, and I'd sit on the floor joists in the attic, a scant ten feet above her, and listen to her cry herself to sleep. And every night, I wondered what it would be like to have a relationship with a woman of such passion. Yes, she cussed like a sailor! Yes, she was often cold and unfeeling and could turn into the world's biggest bitch in the blink of an eye. And yes, she was everything I look for in a woman. Taming a woman like Rachel, capturing her heart, making her crave me would be like reaching the summit of Kilimanjaro. I pictured winning her over, making her want to do things to me she'd never done to a man, things she'd never dreamed of doing.

I knew exactly what to do, which buttons to push, which words to say.

But I waited too long.

And Kevin Vaughn beat me to it.

I could have had her; there's not an ounce of doubt in my mind.

But Kevin Vaughn got her. He caught her at the exact moment in her life, and he won her over and got her to do all the sick, twisted, sexy, passionate, loving things I'd dreamed of her doing to me.

I'm bullshitting you. I'm Kevin Vaughn.

Chapter 35

TO BE PRECISE, Rachel knows me as Kevin Vaughn. My idea was to take the remaining fifty million dollars I had and put it into a corporation. This is a sum of money the government would feel good about confiscating someday, so I figured I may as well make it easy for them to find. I had our geek squad do a patent search for anything related to health or healthy lifestyles, Rachel's specialty. It took a couple of months, but they located a home fitness product that had a chance to sell enough units to actually turn a profit. I also put a few hundred thousand into a webzine that had a small but powerful subscriber base. Then I brought these products to Rachel's company and asked to see examples of work produced by the various account reps.

Naturally, I loved Rachel's work and surprised everyone by insisting she lead the team to overhaul my webzine and promote my fitness product. This appreciation of her skill was like catnip to a kitten for an underappreciated wife in the death throes of her marriage.

Big-budget advertising requires a lot of initial face time between the ad coordinator and the company rep. It thoroughly impressed Rachel, as well as her company, that I involved myself personally in the meetings.

And there were lots of meetings, lots of late-nighters.

I should mention I'm extremely good-looking.

I say this sincerely, as a matter of fact, with no conceit. You can ask anyone—or if you want, just look at me.

Before you judge me for these comments, you should be aware I take no pride in my looks. They're not mine, after all. They're the result of a total facial reconstruction by the top plastic surgeons in the world, a procedure that left me with movie-star looks. I didn't ask for these looks, and I don't like them. They were forced on me by the Agency while I was in a coma. Everything from the tip of my head to the base of my neck began as a fantasy in the minds of the world's greatest plastic surgeons. The coma lasted three years, during which time, I had the opportunity to heal in an antiseptic, controlled environment. I've been told there has never been a more successful plastic surgery performed and probably such a surgery will never be performed again.

I took my time with Rachel. My flirting was subtle, just enough to pique her interest, not enough to cause alarm. There was no sexual pressure. I knew I couldn't push her and didn't need to. I'd seen her naked hundreds of times over the previous fifteen months, so I was in no hurry to get her clothes off—which made me that much more appealing to her.

She'd never met anyone as understanding as me, as wealthy, or as good-looking (I know, I know. But these were her words, not mine). I never spoke ill of her husband, and in the early days, when she brought his name up, I changed the subject.

This was not about sex or lust or power or control or any of those things—not completely any of those things. It was more about Rachel being the kind of woman that fits my biological imperative. Millions of years of gene programming led me to be attracted to a certain type of woman.

Actually, that's a crock, since I'm attracted to most types of women. But women like Rachel give me reason to care.

My job precludes normal, healthy relationships. I've been married once (Janet) and have a wonderful daughter (Kimberly). I fell in love about five years ago, just before the coma (Kathleen), but the Agency told everyone I'd died and had a mock funeral for me. Kathleen, thinking I was dead, fell in love with the next guy who came along, and married him. Most of the years before and after Kathleen were spent in the company of hookers, several of whom have become close friends.

Janet was far too bitchy, Kathleen far too sweet. Rachel's a happy medium.

Our first time?

Well, our first time was tentative. She wanted me to make the first move. I did. Then I pulled back, and she pushed things further. Then she pulled back, and I advanced. We continued this push-me-pull-you dance until we had expended ourselves completely.

Then she looked into my eyes and said, "This can never happen again."

"It won't," I said. "I promise."

Thirty minutes later, we were all over each other, and this time, nothing was tentative. It was as if the floodgates had burst and all her pent-up passion could finally be released.

Chapter 36

THAT WAS SIX months ago. And we've grown closer ever since. I'm not kidding. I'm crazy about her.

A couple of months into the relationship, she told me she planned to divorce Sam. I strongly discouraged it, for two reasons. First, from day one, I'd told Rachel I have no interest in living with or marrying anyone ever again (of course, she feels she'll be able to change my mind). Second, I told her she couldn't afford a divorce because virtually all of Sam's income is off the books.

As for not wanting to live with or marry her, that has nothing to do with Rachel and everything to do with my job. I kill people for a living. If my enemies found out about Rachel, her life would be in constant danger. As for Sam's income being off the books, I have an obvious conflict of interest: if the authorities dig into Sam's activities, they might eventually find my money and seize it.

This topic consumed many hours of our conversation, and I began wondering if there might be another way to solve Rachel's dilemma. If I could find a way to rob Sam's clients, I could siphon off enough money to make Rachel financially independent. Then she could afford to leave Sam without making any demands on his income. I got with Victor, and he surprised me by insisting we hire a team of former FBI profilers to do a psychological evaluation on Sam in order to decide how best to deal with him.

Between Lou Kelly and me, we had reams of information on Sam, enough to get a definitive conclusion by the profilers.

Their conclusion was you don't torture a left-brain genius guy like Sam. His personality is fragile, and he could go into a meltdown and become completely unresponsive.

"This kind of guy is very unique," the head profiler told me. "He's one in a hundred million, which is how he was able to develop this type of computer program in the first place."

"So how do we get him to reveal sensitive information?" I said.

"The best way is to short-circuit his brain."

"Come again?"

"Sam Case is an extreme detail guy. You're going to want to throw as much at him as you can. Hit him with circular references and things that make no sense. Put him on sensory overload. Confuse him. Put him in unfamiliar situations."

"Give him a complete mind fuck?" I said.

"Precisely."

I lined up Callie Carpenter to be his girlfriend, which took a hell of a lot longer than we intended. Sam being a workaholic, we couldn't find a plausible way for them to "meet." In the meantime, Callie established her identity as Karen Vogel. With our Agency connections, she managed to get a Kentucky driver's license, Social Security card, and several credit cards. Then she got a job and a checking account and bought a condo in Karen's name. She made the connection with Mary's friend and co-worker, Chuck.

While all this was going on, Victor and I assembled the team and equipment we would need to put Sam's brain into overload.

Finally, five weeks ago, we managed to get Karen and Sam in the same place at the same time in a plausible scenario that allowed Callie to manipulate him into making his move. The rest, as they say, is history.

Then we had Karen break the news about Rachel's affair to Chuck, who told Mary. At first, Mary didn't believe it, so she followed us to a hotel one night. Mary, protective big sister that she was, gave Rachel an ultimatum: confess the affair to Sam, or she would. Mary and Rachel argued back and forth for several days, and as the anger escalated, the fights became heated. And one day, without any input from me, my friend Salvatore Bonadello, crime boss of the Midwestern United States, got a call from a woman named Rachel Case of Louisville, Kentucky.

Rachel wanted to know how to go about hiring a hit man to kill her sister.

You could have knocked me over with a feather! My intention had been to have Mary meet Sam and tell him about the affair. Then we were going to orchestrate an entire drama around his trying to catch Rachel in the act. We had all sorts of twists and turns to confuse him.

But Rachel had taken things into her own hands.

I told Sal to let it slide. The original plan would work, and no one had to die. Sal wanted the forty grand he was going to charge Rachel for the hit. He wanted me to take the contract and split the fee. I told him if he insisted on killing Rachel's sister, he'd have to cut the fee to twenty grand and we'd give the entire sum to Jimmy Squint, because I didn't want Rachel to pay any more than she had to. Sal is not the sort to leave money on the table, but after I reminded him that his take of the heist would be five hundred million dollars, he reluctantly agreed to the twenty g's.

Karen told Chuck that Rachel's boyfriend was unstable and that he might harm Mary if she met with Sam. She thought Sam and Mary should meet in a public place, like Seneca Park, and Sam shouldn't know what the meeting was about beforehand. Karen said she'd talk to Sam and make sure he showed.

At the last minute, Chuck talked Mary into letting him come to the meeting at the park. He had an authentic police uniform he'd bought for a costume party and felt that wearing the uniform might discourage Rachel's unstable boyfriend from making a scene—which is why the twenty grand suddenly had to cover two killings instead of one. Jimmy Squint didn't mind. He was in the middle of a financial drought and thankful to get whatever I could give him.

We planned for Sam's meeting with Mary to coincide with Sam's first sexual encounter with Karen. This was simple to arrange, since Karen controlled both the meeting with Mary and the hotel room with Sam.

Rachel and I explored all realms of her sexuality, and I found a use for the photograph I had taken of her rape fantasy several months ago, where she pretended to be tied down in her bra and panties. I drew the "K" and "V" on her cups with a marker to identify her as my property, and later on, when making the decision to rob Sam's clients, I gave Callie the name Karen Vogel in order to match the initials.

As we got close to the big event, Sal Bonadello learned his part, and we hired some grifters to play the parts of Aiden Fry and the other camera crew members. We rehearsed in the underground parking lot Victor had purchased.

Speaking of Victor, he always goes all out with these productions. I assured him that all we had to do was build a few soundproof cells in his parking garage. But he had this wild idea of building soundproofed Lucite containers, equipping them with vacuum pumps, and fitting them to flatbed trucks! He barely got the trucks finished in time, but I never doubted he would, having worked with him successfully several times in the past.

Then, with everyone and everything in place, we decided to give Sam a proper mind fuck.

The wild card was Rachel. We had no idea how she would react to being kidnapped. I was concerned about her, so Lou (the voice Sam and Rachel would hear in their cells) kept me constantly informed as to her physical and emotional state.

I had a bit of trepidation allowing Callie and me to be placed into the Lucite containers, so I had prearranged a number of safeguards with Lou Kelly, Callie, Sal Bonadello, and even Victor. You can never be certain about the people working a heist with you, but I figured with so much money to share, we'd be able to trust each other. Plus, we had a history of working together, and that counts for a lot.

From the moment Rachel and Sam were locked in Lucite, I was able to hear everything they said and heard. The only thing I didn't get to see was Callie getting naked for Sam. I've known Callie a third of her life, and I can tell you, I'm jealous that Sam managed to bang my ultimate fantasy girl, something I've never managed to do.

Not that it matters, and it's not even relative to the discussion, but Callie's a lesbian. She has a wonderful live-in relationship with a female trapeze artist in Las Vegas, so I know it wasn't easy for her to sneak away for three months and seduce Sam Case.

Actually, it wasn't *that* hard. Callie's hopelessly in love with her girlfriend, Eva LeSage, but I expect she'd seduce a rabid grizzly bear for a billion dollars.

I know I would.

Which brings us to the present, where Sam, Rachel, and I are in our containers, and Rachel has just chosen me to live and sentenced her husband to die. I'm dressed in a business suit, pretending to be Kevin Vaughn, and Sam is pretending he doesn't know I'm Donovan Creed.

Chapter 37

I ADMIT RACHEL'S attitude toward Sam is giving me pause.

I've always said the way to really know a woman is to lock her in a cage and poke her with a stick. This isn't quite the same, but it's close. And what I've learned about my girlfriend, Rachel, during this short period of captivity is revealing and more than a little disturbing. Starting with the obvious, she doesn't appear to be an overly compassionate person. Her colorful vocabulary could benefit from a makeover. The fact that she was entirely convincing when begging Sam to choose her over Karen tells me she's not just a capable liar but probably a pathological one as well. Her ability to be completely sensual and loving one moment and capable of murdering her sister or husband the next suggests an undiagnosed schizophrenic personality disorder.

Then again, I kill people for a living, so which of us is perfect?

I'm crazy about Rachel. And while *crazy* might be the operative word, I'm already looking forward to seeing how we click when it's just the two of us living in her attic.

Okay, so let me catch you up in real time: Lou Kelly (the voice) has just said, "Sorry for the delay. We're good to go. Make your peace, Sam. I'll give you ten seconds."

Sam said, "You get nine billion dollars, and I get ten seconds, huh?"

Lou: "Doesn't hardly seem fair, does it?"

Sam: "When does the countdown begin?"

Lou: "Now ... unless anyone has a final comment ... No? In that case—"

I clear my throat and say, "Actually, if I may, I'd like to ask Sam a quick question."

Sam looks up at me. So does Rachel. She looks worried and says, "Kevin, we're so close. Please, hon, let's just end this and go home."

Sam says to me, "What's your question?"

I answer, "Did you type my code last?"

Rachel says, "What?"

"It was all happening so fast," Sam says, "but yes. I entered your code last, like we discussed."

"Good man."

Rachel begins screaming incoherently, something about, "You know him? What the hell is going on here? What the fuck does this mean? Answer me! Answer me, you son of a bitch—" That sort of thing.

I turn to her, knowing what to look for. If there's one thing I've learned about dating relationships, it's that being able to predict your partner's moods is of paramount importance. In Rachel's case (pardon the play on words), her face is her barometer, so I am reassured to see her neck, ears, and face gaining color quickly. I've noticed her face only turns crimson when she's furious or craving sex, and I've been teaching myself to know which is which. It's these little things you learn about the people you're dating that mean so much down the road.

I let her yammer on awhile before focusing on her husband.

"Sam," I say, "There's no way to dance around the issue. I'm in love with your wife."

Rachel immediately stops screaming. "What? Wait—did you just say you're in love with me?"

I smile. "I am. Hopelessly."

She settles down and places her hand on the glass in a loving manner, while her face remains bright red. See what I mean? From furious to sensual in nothing flat—what a woman!

Sam says, "I find that impossible to believe."

Rachel says, "Shut up, Sam. Shut up and die."

Like I said, Rachel ain't perfect.

Sam says, "Rachel, you might want to ask Kevin what his real name is."

I say, "Sam, with all due respect, that's a matter between Rachel and me."

"Fuck you both," he says.

"Sam, I was hoping we could all leave here as friends."

He looks at me as if I come from another dimension, a place where we all look normal, but nothing we say makes sense.

"Friends? You want to be friends?"

I nod.

"Let's see if I've got this right," he says. "I agreed to protect your blood money. In return, you broke into my house, hacked into my computer, monitored my every move, fucked my wife, set me up with a hooker, drugged and kidnapped me twice, murdered my wife's sister and at least one innocent man, kept me and my wife imprisoned for two days, nearly killing Rachel in the process, forced me to sentence Karen to die, stole more than nine billion dollars from my clients—which means even if you let me go, my life expectancy is now what, three days? Wait, don't answer. I'm not finished. You put me out of business, put me through mental and physical anguish, forced me to learn my wife has been having a six-month affair with my own client, made me endure the humiliation of having my own wife sentence me to die, and now you tell me you're in love with my wife and plan to take her away from me, but you want us to be friends?"

"Yes, that's it," I say. "Except for the part about physical anguish. I think that's a bit hyperbolic."

"You do," he says.

I nod.

"But other than that?"

"I'd say you have a good grasp on it. Except for one thing."

"What's that?"

"I'm going to give you a quarter billion of the take."

"Big deal. I'll be dead within days."

"I'll help you get a new face, new identity, and a new life."

"With Karen Vogel?"

"Get real, son."

"Okay," he says. "I'll take it."

"Lou," I say, "open the containers and let's wrap things up. Rachel and I have a lot to talk about."

Nothing happens.

"Lou?"

Chapter 38

SOME TIME GOES by.

Too much time.

Finally, Lou says, "Uh, Donovan? We never talked about Sam getting a quarter billion dollars."

"I'm giving it to him out of my part. I'm giving Rachel twenty-five million as well."

Rachel looks at me and smiles.

"Thank you, Kevin," she says.

I smile back.

Lou says, "We haven't really discussed this, but do you think you could get out of that cage without my help?"

I say, "Lou, we've been together a long time."

"True," he says. "But your share is weighing heavy on me right now. Not saying I'm ungrateful or anything, but five hundred million dollars seemed a lot bigger to me when this plan was first hatched."

"Half a billion dollars seems small to you?"

"Compared to you getting six times as much, and Sam getting half as much, and both of you being in a cage and all."

"You figure to kill me and take my three billion?"

"I feel terrible about it," Lou says. "You know I've always been a team player, but I've got two monitors in front of me. One shows three containers with helpless people inside. The other shows more than nine billion dollars sitting in a bank account, waiting to be accessed. I can't help but notice that two clicks would change everything. One click and the vacuum pumps kill you in five minutes. A click on the bank account and your share—three billion dollars—goes into my personal account, along with the half billion we talked about."

"Lou, I'm disappointed in you."

"I was disappointed in you a couple years back, when you killed your best friend. I can only wonder how quickly you'd put a bullet in my head if I ever displeased you."

"That's totally unrelated, and you know it. You're rationalizing."

"Maybe so, but I guess it takes a certain amount of rationalizing to turn my back on the man who's saved my life several times."

"Don't let that part weigh on you," I say. "You've saved my life too."

"Thanks for acknowledging it."

I keep my voice even. "Lou, if it helps you decide, I guarantee I can get out of this cage in less than five minutes."

He pauses a full minute, weighing my words. "I don't think so," he says. "I've gone over this a hundred times in my head. I spent several hours in one of the units the other day and tried to find a way out. There was none. Victor does great work, you know that."

"You think Victor's going to let you walk with my share? Or Sal?"

"No. But I think if you're dead, they'd each take a billion not to come after me."

"I'm not even dead yet, and the three billion you're stealing is already down to one."

"True," Lou says. "But it's still three times as much as I've got now. Every time I tell myself this is a horrible thing to do, I realize I can triple my take by pressing two buttons."

"What about the midgets?"

"They're on break until I tell them to come back and drive. I'm good for at least an hour."

"You're all alone?"

"All alone and getting greedier by the minute."

"Victor is monitoring everything you're doing," I say.

"He was until I cut his live feed a couple of minutes ago."

"Don't do it, Lou."

"I can't help myself. I wish I could."

"Will you at least set Sam and Rachel free?"

"No. It's got to be all or none."

Rachel says, "Kevin?"

"Not now, hon, I'm kind of busy."

I know the clock is running. Every second counts. I kick off my shoes and pry the heels off. I catch Lou off guard, but he recovers quickly. He throws the switch, and the vacuum pump comes on in my cell.

Chapter 39

I PULL THE plastic explosives from the hollowed-out heels of my shoes, pull off my suit jacket, and remove my shirt and tie. I remove the wires from my shirt collar, where you'd normally find the collar stays.

Rachel says, "Kevin!"

"Not now, sweetheart," I say. "But don't worry. I'll get you out in a couple of minutes."

"You promise?"

I stop working for a second. I need to think it through. I take my promises seriously. I perform some calculations in my head.

"Kevin?" she says.

"Yes," I say. "I promise I'll save you."

"Thank you. I love you."

"Love you too."

I place one of the charges above the check valve in the floor, the one that allows the air to flow in one direction at a time. I uncoil ten feet of the detonator wire I'd taken from one of my collars and push it into place.

Sam says, "Not to interrupt, but what about me?"

I stop long enough to look at him. Poor Sam, always sucking hind tit. Then again, he had sex with Callie, so he's already gotten his break in life.

"Sorry, Sam, I've only got two charges."

He nods and says, "Typical."

The vacuum pump is doing its job, but it is at least a minute away from affecting me.

"Hey, Rachel?" I say.

"Yes?"

"Tell me when your pump comes on, okay?"

"Uh, it's been on about thirty seconds."

Shit!

"Really?"

"Really. Is that okay?"

I try to sound cheerful. "That's perfect," I say.

"See you soon then."

"Okay."

"Can't hardly wait," she says.

I grab the cooler, lift the lid, and check for the little hole in the hinge I'd told Victor to install as a last resort, the one that covered the blasting cap. I find it, run the detonator wire through it, and wad up the balance of the wire to create extra friction. I slam the lid shut, creating enough energy to set off the chemical reaction.

The blast is instantaneous, and everything I'm about to tell you takes place in a half second. But here's how it works: When the chemical reaction begins, C-4 decomposes to release nitrogen and carbon oxides. The gases expand over 26,000 feet per second, applying trauma force to anything in the immediate area.

That's why I used such a small amount of C-4, just enough to do the job, not enough to blow myself to hell.

A C-4 explosion has two phases. In the first phase, the initial explosion blows the check valve open, rendering the vacuum pump ineffective. This phase creates an extreme low-pressure area at the point of origin which blows the gases outward, lifts me off my feet, and hurls me toward the back wall. In phase two, a millisecond later, the gases rush back into the partial vacuum, creating a second, less-destructive inward energy wave, sufficient to implode the Lucite walls, one of which knocks me to the floor and nearly renders me unconscious. My ears are ringing from the explosion, but I manage to hear something that sounds like Rachel's voice.

"Oh my God, Kevin, are you all right?" Rachel says.

I'm not—not yet. But my speakers are blown, so how the hell can I hear her?

"Kevin? Kevin!"

"His name's Donovan Creed," Sam says.

"Fuck you, Sam!" Rachel says. Then she shouts, "You're all right! Thank God! I see you moving!"

I am all right, but why am I able to hear everyone? Lou must be on the run, must have turned on the speakers throughout the garage so he could hear what was going on as he made his escape—unless he's coming after me with a gun to finish me off!

No. Lou wouldn't take that big of a chance. He knows the trucks have pump-action shotguns in the cabs.

I work my way out of the cage, not an easy thing to do with a thick wall of Lucite on my back. I look around. Unfortunately, I can't find the rest of the plastic explosive. It has been knocked from my hand. I could probably find it eventually, but I've also lost the second detonator wire.

I have to save Rachel, but I have nothing to work with.

She picks up on my expression. Her eyes grow wide with terror. *Wait*, I think. *The truck!*

I jump into the cab of Rachel's truck, roll down both windows, and fire it up. These things aren't built for speed, and it takes me most of the parking lot to get above twenty miles an hour. By then, I am closing in on the far wall quickly. I make a hairpin turn and manage to miss the wall. But that's not what I'm hoping for. I'm trying to flip the truck onto its side. I get the truck turned around and head back in the direction we'd started in, only now I am up to thirty. I cut the steering wheel, trying to jackknife the cargo area. Two of the wheels come up slightly, but the truck rocks back into place.

Damn!

I turn again, heading back to the far wall. I cut the wheel sharply one way and then the other. Finally, the truck lurches. I slam on the brake, and it continues pitching over onto its side. While bracing myself for the impact, I pray Rachel will survive the crash.

The truck rests on the driver's side with the passenger side straight up. I grab the shotgun from under the seat, push it through the open window, and climb out after it. I jump to the parking lot floor, grab the shotgun, and run to the back of the truck to make sure Rachel is alive.

She is!

I motion her to make her way to the back of the truck. She does. I motion her to stay there. Then I walk back to the side where the bottom of the truck is exposed and find the check valve. I pump a shell into the chamber, back up a few yards, and fire into the valve at an angle, hoping not to catch any shrapnel from the ricochet. The valve blows open. I take a deep breath. Rachel is safe.

I turn my attention to Sam. He's lying on the floor unconscious. But at least he's lying at the far side of the check valve. I know I don't have enough time to flip his truck. I pump another round into the shotgun, climb under the truck, place the barrel against the check valve, and wedge the shotgun into place.

I can only think of one way to pull the trigger without getting seriously injured or killed from the shell rebound.

I remove my belt and wedge the buckle under the trigger. It doesn't quite reach the side of the truck, which means it's still too dangerous. I take off my pants, tie one leg around the belt, and hold on to the end of the other pant leg. I climb onto the narrow ledge on the side of the truck and pull the pant leg as hard as I can.

The shotgun fires.

I jump down and climb under the truck to inspect my work. And see a nice-sized hole where the check valve used to be.

If Sam is still alive, he'll be okay soon.

I leave my belt but grab my pants, climb into Sam's truck, buckle up, and head for the garage door at full speed, which is about thirty. But it's enough to break through, and within minutes, I'm in the control room with my pants on. Since the containers were built to open from the very back, neither has suffered any damage. I press a button on the console and pop them both open. Then I walk back to check on my girlfriend and her husband.

Chapter 40

SAM IS CLOSER, so I start with him. I climb into the cubicle and hoist him out. He is unconscious but breathing, so I lay him out on the floor and go to get Rachel. She meets me halfway, and we do that movie thing where we run to each other from opposite directions and embrace when we meet. She actually squeals and jumps into my arms, and I think of Lula and Sailor in *Wild at Heart*.

By the time we get back to the room where I'd set Sam down, he is gone.

I know where he'll be.

Rachel and I continue to the control room where I'd gone moments earlier to set them free. Sam is so out of it he is fairly swooning, but he sits at the computer, trying to track the money.

When Rachel and I approach, he gives her a withering look. She stiffens and leans into my side.

"I love him, Sam. You're just going to have to deal with it," Rachel says.

Sam ignores the remark, proving he'd rather lose Rachel than the money.

"Nothing makes sense," he says. "My Web site's totally trashed. I see the money in an account, but it's an account I've never seen. I keep trying to access the funds, but the screen remains unchanged."

"That's Lou Kelly's bank account," I say. "The screen is locked on it."

"So you've lost your money," he says, "which means I've lost mine."

"Kevin," Rachel says, "I'd rather have you than twenty-five million any day!"

"For the love of God," Sam says, rolling his eyes.

Rachel is about to respond, and if she'd had the chance, I would have expected some cussing to pass her lips. But she sees what we all see on one of the security monitors: someone approaching the front door.

Lou Kelly comes in first, followed closely by Callie, who has Lou's jacket draped over her shoulder. Lou's arms are behind his back, which tells me Callie has twist-tied his wrists with plastic.

"It's Karen!" Sam says.

Rachel's back seems to arch. "I don't want her here!" she says.

"Relax," I say. "She's bringing Lou back."

"Could be a trap," Sam says. "He's twice her size. What're the chances she got the drop on him?"

"A hundred percent," I say. "Lou's a good hand, but he's older and partially paralyzed on his left side. Callie knows that."

Sam sets his jaw.

I say, "Tread lightly, Sam. Callie will fuck you up."

"Yeah? Well, I'm not old or paralyzed," he says.

We watch them on the bank of monitors. Callie nudges Lou into the hallway. Lou isn't fighting her over it. As they're about to enter the war room where we stand watching them, I say, "Be nice. Both of you."

"But, Kevin," Rachel whines.

"I mean it. You and Callie are going to be friends."

"Fat chance," Rachel says. "Fucking whore."

"For once, we agree," Sam says.

I give Rachel a look that makes her wince. She says, "Sorry, Kevin. I'll try."

"See that you do."

Lou and Callie approach.

"Lou," I say.

"Donovan."

After a moment of us looking at each other, I say, "What was that all about, Lou?"

He presses his lips together tightly, then opens them, and takes a breath. "Ah, shit, Donovan. I can't explain it. I would have bet I was a better person than that."

I nod.

Lou says, "By the way, that was incredible."

"My escape?"

"Looked like the old days, back in Europe. I should have left sooner, but I just had to watch, you know? It was like watching a movie."

"Like *Rambo* or something?"

"Yeah. Like that."

"The critics panned those shows," I say. "But they were entertaining."

"Sly's one-dimensional," Lou says. "But if a guy's entertaining enough, one dimension's all you need."

I pause. "About the money ..."

"I want to make it right," Lou says. "I know things will never be the same between us, but I want to put the finances back like they were. Let me go and I'll transfer the full three to your account."

"Before the heist, I started with two-fifty of my own," I say.

"I thought that was part of the three," Lou says.

"Nope. Same with Victor. We both had two-fifty in. We get that back first, then the split."

"If I knew that, I would have tried to shoot you!" Lou says.

"Lucky me."

He chuckles.

Sam and Rachel look at Callie. Callie puts her hand out to Rachel. Rachel looks at me. I nod. Rachel approaches Callie and embraces her. "I'm sorry I called you a whore," she says.

Callie bristles. "You probably should have kept that remark to yourself."

"Well, you did sleep with her husband," I say.

Callie says, "We can get past that." She smiles at me and says, "You've got your hands full with this one."

Sam says, "Hey, Karen, how about a quick fuck before you hit the road?"

I kneel down and lift Sam's head off the floor so he won't choke on his own blood. Callie hands me Lou's jacket and I stuff it under Sam's head.

To Callie, Rachel says, "What did you hit him with? I never saw you move a muscle."

Callie looks at her but says nothing. Rachel steps slightly behind me to make herself less of a target—just in case.

Lou says to Rachel, "You can see why I surrendered so easily."

"Lou," I say again. "About the money ..."

Chapter 41

LOU SAYS, "I can put it back. Three point two-five billion. Take me thirty seconds. But I need your word."

One of Sam's fingers starts twitching.

"That's a good sign," I say.

Callie says, "You have a reason to want him alive? Because the only way I can get the stench off me is to end the memory."

"I might have a use for him," I say.

Callie cocks her head at me. "My understanding was Sam wasn't coming out of the cage alive."

"Look at him," I say. "Guy's lost his wife, his job. Don't you think he's been through enough?"

Callie gives me a puzzled look. In front of my chest, where Rachel can't see, I point my thumb toward myself and move it slightly to indicate Rachel. Callie picks up on it and nods.

"Fine," she says. "We'll keep him alive then."

"I might have a use for him," I repeat.

"He's got a mouth on him, though," Callie says.

"I think you solved that problem already."

To Lou, I say, "We've been through a lot, and like you said before, I'm running out of friends. We can't work together anymore, but I'm willing to let you walk out of here and build a life."

"Thank you, Donovan. I'll transfer the money as soon as I get some distance between us," he says.

"I'll trust you to do it," I say.

He nods.

He hesitates.

"I have your word on this, right?" he says.

"You do."

He looks at Callie. "Are we going to have a problem?"

She looks at me and then back at Lou. "I guess not. Looks like everyone gets a free pass today."

"Thanks, guys," Lou says. "Old times, huh?"

"Old times," I say.

"Uh ... if it's not too much trouble ..." Lou says.

With a quickness to rival Jimmy Squint, Callie produces a knife. She cuts him loose from his plastic twist ties, and Lou walks away.

Rachel says, "You trust that guy to wire three billion to your account?"

I laugh. "I think if he had the money he would."

"He doesn't have the money?" Callie says.

Sam is still unconscious, but his arm is jerking in a strange motion above his chest, as though he were swatting flies in slow motion.

I say, "Remember how I told Sam to enter my code last?"

Callie nods.

"As you know, Victor is a computer genius too. He's been working with Sam's Web site for months. He couldn't access the accounts without the names, but he reset all the data parameters. All the funds went to the last account entered."

"But Lou said he personally put the money in his account," Rachel says.

"This computer had nothing to do with the accounts," I say. "That's why Sam couldn't make it work a few minutes ago. Lou was inputting data directly onto Victor's computer screen, not the bank's. We wouldn't have trusted anyone with nine billion dollars and a keystroke. Not even Lou Kelly."

"So he never saw the money at all," Callie says. "The nine billion was just a made-up number?"

I nod. "It's a close estimate. We won't know how much there is until I access my account. That's where the money is."

"Victor trusts you to do the right thing?" Callie says.

"Wouldn't you?"

"I would," she says. "You may be a killer, but you're not a crook."

From behind me, Rachel pipes up. "Kevin is *not* a killer. He's the nicest man I know."

Callie says, "You poor thing."

I kneel back down and check Sam's pulse. To Rachel, I say, "He's going to be all right. You want to go home now?"

She looks puzzled. "You mean we get to keep the house?"

I smile. "To pack some clothes. We're going on vacation."

"What about my job?"

"You're quitting."

"But—"

"Come here a sec. I want to show you something."

I sit at the computer, log into the Citizen's Bank Web page, and type in an account number. Rachel's name comes up.

"That's my name," she says. "But I don't bank there."

"I opened this account for you," I say, pulling up her balance. "Check it out."

"Twenty-five million dollars?"

I nod.

"Oh ... my ... *God!*"

She starts dancing around the room, hopping up and down and squealing like a banshee with her first orgasm. While she does that, I access my account and check the last deposit.

"Nine billion seven hundred million and change," I say.

"Nice haul," Callie says.

"You and Eva have plans for spending it?"

"Not yet. We'll kick back and enjoy our life awhile."

"How many years can she perform?"

"Solo trapeze? If she stays injury free, one, maybe two more years."

"She won't stay on after she gets demoted?"

Callie smiles. "She won't need to, now."

Rachel's pirouette ends. She kisses my cheek and says, "I love you, Kevin."

"Does that mean you'll vacation with me?"

"Can I bring my sex toys?"

"That's my girl!"

Sam starts coming to.

"Will he be okay?" Rachel asks.

"I think so. Just to be safe, I'll have Callie take him to a hospital."

"Thanks, Callie," Rachel says.

"My pleasure," Callie says, sweetly.

Then she and I exchange a knowing look.

11516382R0013

Made in the USA
Lexington, KY
18 October 2011